*Acclaim for Toni Morrison's* **JAZZ**

"Marvelous. . . . Morrison is perhaps the finest novelist of our time."
—*Vogue*

"The author conjures up worlds with complete authority and makes no secret of her angst at the injustices dealt to black women." —Edna O'Brien, *The New York Times Book Review*

"She captures that almost indistinguishable mixture of the anxiety and rapture of expectation—that state of desire where sin is just another word for appetite." —*San Francisco Chronicle*

"As rich in themes and poetic images as her Pulitzer Prize–winning *Beloved*. . . . Morrison conjures up the hand of slavery on Harlem's jazz generation. The more you listen, the more you crave to hear."
—*Glamour*

"She is the best writer in America. Jazz, for sure; but also Mozart." —John Leonard, National Public Radio

"A masterpiece. . . . A sensuous, haunting story of various kinds of passion. . . . Mesmerizing." —*Cosmopolitan*

"Lyrically brooding. . . . One accepts the characters of *Jazz* as generalized figures moving rhythmically in the narrator's mind."
—*The New York Times*

"Transforms a familiar refrain of jilted love into a bold, sustaining time of self-knowledge and discovery. Its rhythms are infectious."
—*People*

ALSO BY TONI MORRISON

FICTION

*Love*

*Paradise*

*Beloved*

*Tar Baby*

*Song of Solomon*

*Sula*

*The Bluest Eye*

NONFICTION

*The Dancing Mind*

*Playing in the Dark:*
*Whiteness and the Literary Imagination*

Toni Morrison

# JAZZ

Toni Morrison is the Robert F. Goheen Professor of Humanities, Emeritus at Princeton University. She has received the National Book Critics Circle Award and the Pulitzer Prize. In 1993 she was awarded the Nobel Prize in Literature. She lives in Rockland County, New York, and Princeton, New Jersey.

# JAZZ

# JAZZ

*a novel*

Toni Morrison

Vintage International
Vintage Books
A Division of Random House, Inc.
New York

FIRST VINTAGE INTERNATIONAL EDITION, JUNE 2004

*Copyright © 1992, 2004 by Toni Morrison*

All rights reserved under International and Pan-American Copyright Conventions.
Published in the United States by Vintage Books, a division of Random House, Inc., New York, and simultaneously in Canada by Random House of Canada Limited, Toronto. Originally published in slightly different form in hardcover in the United States by Alfred A. Knopf, a division of Random House, Inc., New York, in 1992.

Vintage is a registered trademark and Vintage International and colophon are trademarks of Random House, Inc.

The Library of Congress has cataloged the Knopf edition as follows:
Morrison, Toni.
Jazz / Toni Morrison.
p. cm.
1. African Americans—Fiction. 2. Crimes of passion—Fiction. 3. Middle aged persons—Fiction. 4. Funeral rites and ceremonies—Fiction. 5. Triangles (Interpersonal relations)—Fiction. 6. Harlem (New York, N.Y.)—Fiction. 7. Psychological fiction. 8. Historical fiction. I. Title.
PS3563.08749 J38 1992
813'.54—dc20
91-58555

**Vintage ISBN:** 1-4000-7621-8

www.vintagebooks.com

Printed in the United States of America
20 19 18

for R W

and

George

I am the name of the sound
    and the sound of the name.
I am the sign of the letter
    and the designation of the division.

"Thunder, Perfect Mind,"
*The Nag Hammadi*

# FOREWORD

"She stood there licking snowflakes from her top lip, her body shaking everywhere except the left hand which held the knife . . ."

It didn't work, this opening sentence to *Jazz,* because it made what could follow mechanical and predictable: the inevitability of "Then she . . ." seemed inappropriate for this project. I was interested in rendering a period in African American life through a specific lens—one that would reflect the content and characteristics of its music (romance, freedom of choice, doom, seduction, anger) and the manner of its expression. I had decided on the period, the narrative line, and the place long ago, after seeing a photograph of a pretty girl in a coffin, and reading the photographer's recollection of how she got there. In the book *The Harlem Book of the Dead,* the photographer, James Van Der Zee, tells Camille Billops what he remembers of the girl's death: "She was the one I think was shot by her sweetheart at a party with a noiseless gun. She complained of being sick at the party and friends said, 'Well, why don't you lay down?' And they took her in the room and laid her down. After they undressed her and loosened her clothes, they saw the blood on her dress. They asked her about it and she said, 'I'll tell you tomorrow, yes. I'll tell you tomorrow.' She was just trying to give him a chance to get away. For the picture, I placed the flowers on her chest." Her motives for putting herself at risk by waiting, for accepting a lover's vengeance as legitimate, seemed so young, so foolish, so wrapped up and entangled in the sacrifice that tragically romantic love demanded. The anecdote seemed to me redolent of the proud hopelessness of love mourned and championed in blues music, and, simultaneously, fired by the irresistible energy of jazz music. It asserted itself immediately and aggressively as the seed of a plot, a story line.

*Beloved* unleashed a host of ideas about how and what one cherishes under the duress and emotional disfigurement that a slave society imposes. One such idea—love as perpetual mourning (haunting)—led me to consider a parallel one: how such relationships were altered, later, in (or by) a certain level of liberty. An alteration made abundantly clear in the music. I was struck by the modernity that jazz anticipated and directed, and by its unreasonable optimism. Whatever the truth or consequences of individual entanglements and the racial landscape, the music insisted that the past might haunt us, but it would not entrap us. It demanded a future—and refused to regard the past as ". . . an abused record with no choice but to repeat itself at the crack and no power on earth could lift the arm that held the needle."

For three years the cast had been taking shape—an older couple born in the South; the impact on them of a new urban liberty; the emotional unmanageableness of radical change from the menace of post-Reconstruction South to the promise of post–WWI North. The couple would be forced to respond to a girl who introduces into their lives a new kind of risk—psychological rather than physical. To reproduce the flavor of the period, I had read issues of every "Colored" newspaper I could for the year 1926. The articles, the advertisements, the columns, the employment ads. I had read Sunday School programs, graduation ceremony programs, minutes of women's club meetings, journals of poetry, essays. I listened to the scratchy "race" records with labels like Okeh, Black Swan, Chess, Savoy, King, Peacock.

And I remembered.

My mother was twenty years old in 1926; my father nineteen. Five years later, I was born. They had both left the South as children, chock full of scary stories coupled with a curious nostalgia. They played the records, sang the songs, read the press, wore the clothes, spoke the language of the twenties; debating endlessly the status of The Negro.

I remember opening the metal trunk sitting like a treasure chest in the hall. The lock, clasped shut but not key-locked, was thrilling; its round head, the cylinders—everything fit and clicked and obeyed. The lid was heavy, but silent on its hinges; an appropriately stealthy entrance into this treasure that I have been cautioned never, ever, to approach. I am too young to be in school, and the days are endless without my sister. She is solemn and important, now that she has a daily appointment (first grade) and I have nothing to do. My mother is in the backyard. No one else is in the house, so no one will know how accommodating the lock is, how quietly the lid rises. The treasure I believe is hidden there does not disappoint. Right on top of crepe dresses is an evening purse, tiny, jeweled with fringe dangled in jet and glass.

My mother hears the scream but I don't. I only remember the crack of pain as the trunk lid smashes my hand, then waking up in her arms. I thought she would be angry at me for my disobedience, but she is not. She is soothing, sings a little, as she massages my hand, rubs it with a triangle of ice. I had fainted. What an adult thing to do! How jealous my sister will be when I tell her about the pain, how grown up I felt and how loved. But seeing, examining the purse, the treasure—I would not describe that to her. I would keep this glimpse of my mother's world before I was born to myself. It was private. It was glittery. And now, it was mine as well.

Following *Beloved*'s focus on mother-love, I intended to examine couple-love—the reconfiguration of the "self" in such relationships; the negotiation between individuality and commitment to another. Romantic love seemed to me one of the fingerprints of the twenties, and jazz its engine.

Although I had a concept, its context, a plot line, characters, data, I could not establish the structure where meaning, rather than information, would lie; where the project came as close as it could to its idea of itself—the essence of the so-called Jazz Age. The moment when an African American art form defined, influenced, reflected a nation's culture in so many ways: the bourgeoning of sexual license, a burst of political, economic, and artistic power; the ethical conflicts between the sacred and the secular; the hand of the past being crushed by the present. Primary among these features, however, was invention. Improvisation, originality, change. Rather than be about those characteristics, the novel would seek to become them.

My effort to enter that world was constantly being frustrated. I couldn't locate the voice, or position the eye. The story opened with the betrayed wife intent on killing her rival. "She stood there licking snowflakes from her top lip. . . ." Okay, perhaps. Perhaps. But nothing that could pull from the material or the people the compositional drama of the period, its unpredictability. I knew everything about this wife and, angered by my inability to summon suitable language to reveal her, I threw my pencil on the floor, sucked my teeth in disgust, thinking, "Oh, shoot! What is this? I know that woman. I know her skirt size, what side she sleeps on. I know the name of her hair oil, its scent. . . ." So that's what I wrote, effortlessly without pause, playing, just playing along with the voice, not even considering who the "I" was until it seemed natural, inevitable, that the narrator could—would—parallel and launch the process of invention, of improvisation, of change. Commenting, judging, risking, and learning. I had written novels in which structure was designed to enhance meaning; here the structure would *equal* meaning. The challenge was to expose and bury the artifice and to take practice beyond the rules. I didn't want simply a musical background, or decorative references to it. I wanted the work to be a manifestation of the music's intellect, sensuality, anarchy; its history, its range, and its modernity.

She sang, my mother, the way other people muse. A constant background drift of beautiful sound I took for granted, like oxygen. "Ave Maria, gratia plena . . . I woke up this morning with an awful aching head/My new man has left me just a room and a bed. . . . Precious Lord, lead me on . . . I'm gonna buy me a pistol, just as long as I am tall. . . . L'amour est un oiseau rebel. . . . When the deep purple falls over hazy garden walls . . . I've got a disposition and a way of my own/When my man starts kicking I let him find a new home. . . . Oh, holy night. . . ." Like the music that came to be known as Jazz, she took from everywhere, knew everything—gospel, classic, blues, hymns—and made it her own.

How interesting it would be to raise the atmosphere, choose the palette, plumb the sounds of her young life, and convert it all into language as seductive, as glittery, as an evening purse tucked away in a trunk!

# JAZZ

Sth, I know that woman. She used to live with a flock of birds on Lenox Avenue. Know her husband, too. He fell for an eighteen-year-old girl with one of those deepdown, spooky loves that made him so sad and happy he shot her just to keep the feeling going. When the woman, her name is Violet, went to the funeral to see the girl and to cut her dead face they threw her to the floor and out of the church. She ran, then, through all that snow, and when she got back to her apartment she took the birds from their cages and set them out the windows to freeze or fly, including the parrot that said, "I love you."

The snow she ran through was so windswept she left no footprints in it, so for a time nobody knew exactly where on Lenox Avenue she lived. But, like me, they knew who she was, who she had to be, because they knew that her husband, Joe Trace, was the one who shot the girl. There was never anyone to prosecute him because nobody actually saw him do it, and the dead girl's aunt didn't want to throw money to helpless lawyers or laughing cops when she knew the expense wouldn't improve anything. Besides, she found out that the man who killed her niece cried all day and for him and for Violet that is as bad as jail.

Regardless of the grief Violet caused, her name was brought up at the January meeting of the Salem Women's Club as someone needing assistance, but it was voted down because only prayer—not money—could help her now, because she had a more or less able husband (who needed to stop feeling sorry for himself), and because a man and his family on 134th Street had lost everything in a fire. The Club mobilized itself to come to the burnt-out family's aid and left Violet to figure out on her own what the matter was and how to fix it.

She is awfully skinny, Violet; fifty, but still good looking when she broke up the funeral. You'd think that being thrown out the church would be the end of it—the shame and all—but it wasn't. Violet is mean enough and good looking enough to think that even without hips or youth she could punish Joe by getting herself a boyfriend and letting him visit in her own house. She thought it would dry his tears up and give her some satisfaction as well. It could have worked, I suppose, but the children of suicides are hard to please and quick to believe no one loves them because they are not really here.

Anyway, Joe didn't pay Violet or her friend any notice.

Whether she sent the boyfriend away or whether he quit her, I can't say. He may have come to feel that Violet's gifts were poor measured against his sympathy for the brokenhearted man in the next room. But I do know that mess didn't last two weeks. Violet's next plan—to fall back in love with her husband—whipped her before it got on a good footing. Washing his handkerchiefs and putting food on the table before him was the most she could manage. A poisoned silence floated through the rooms like a big fishnet that Violet alone slashed through with loud recriminations. Joe's daytime listlessness and both their worrying nights must have wore her down. So she decided to love—well, find out about—the eighteen-year-old whose creamy little face she tried to cut open even though nothing would have come out but straw.

Violet didn't know anything about the girl at first except her name, her age, and that she was very well thought of in the legally licensed beauty parlor. So she commenced to gather the rest of the information. Maybe she thought she could solve the mystery of love that way. Good luck and let me know.

She questioned everybody, starting with Malvonne, an upstairs neighbor—the one who told her about Joe's dirt in the first place and whose apartment he and the girl used as a love nest. From Malvonne she learned the girl's address and whose child she was. From the legally licensed beauticians she found out what kind of lip rouge the girl wore; the marcelling iron they used on her (though I suspect that girl didn't need to straighten her hair); the band the girl liked best (Slim Bates' Ebony Keys which is pretty good except for his vocalist who must be his woman since why else would he let her insult his band). And when she was shown how, Violet did the dance steps the dead girl used to do. All that. When she had the steps down pat—her knees just so—everybody, including the ex-boyfriend, got disgusted with her and I can see why. It was like watching an old street pigeon pecking the crust of a sardine sandwich the cats left behind. But Violet was nothing but persistent and no wisecrack or ugly look stopped her. She haunted PS-89 to talk to teachers who knew the girl. JHS-139 too because the girl went there before trudging way over to Wadleigh, since there were no high schools in her district a colored girl could attend. And for a long time she pestered the girl's aunt, a dignified lady who did fine work off and on in the garment district, until the aunt broke down and began to look forward to Violet's visits for a chat about youth and misbehavior. The aunt showed all the dead girl's things to Violet and it became clear to her (as it was to me) that this niece had been hardheaded as well as sly.

One particular thing the aunt showed her, and eventually let Violet keep for a few weeks, was a picture of the girl's face. Not smiling, but alive at least and very bold. Violet had the nerve to put it on the fireplace mantel in her own parlor and both she and Joe looked at it in bewilderment.

It promised to be a mighty bleak household, what with the birds gone and the two of them wiping their cheeks all day, but when spring came to the City Violet saw, coming into the building with an Okeh record under her arm and carrying some stewmeat wrapped in butcher paper, another girl with four marcelled waves on each side of her head. Violet invited her in to examine the record and that's how that scandalizing threesome on Lenox Avenue began. What turned out different was who shot whom.

• • •

# 7

I'm crazy about this City.

Daylight slants like a razor cutting the buildings in half. In the top half I see looking faces and it's not easy to tell which are people, which the work of stonemasons. Below is shadow where any blasé thing takes place: clarinets and lovemaking, fists and the voices of sorrowful women. A city like this one makes me dream tall and feel in on things. Hep. It's the bright steel rocking above the shade below that does it. When I look over strips of green grass lining the river, at church steeples and into the cream-and-copper halls of apartment buildings, I'm strong. Alone, yes, but top-notch and indestructible—like the City in 1926 when all the wars are over and there will never be another one. The people down there in the shadow are happy about that. At last, at last, everything's ahead. The smart ones say so and people listening to them and reading what they write down agree: Here comes the new. Look out. There goes the sad stuff. The bad stuff. The things-nobody-could-help stuff. The way everybody was then and there. Forget that. History is over, you all, and everything's ahead at last. In halls and offices people are sitting around thinking future thoughts about projects and bridges and fast-clicking trains underneath. The A&P hires a colored clerk. Big-legged women with pink kitty tongues roll money into green tubes for later on; then they laugh and put their arms around each other. Regular people corner thieves in alleys for quick retribution and, if he is stupid and has robbed wrong, thieves corner him too. Hoodlums hand out goodies, do their best to stay interesting, and since they are being watched for excitement, they pay attention to their clothes and the carving out of insults. Nobody wants to be an emergency at Harlem Hospital but if the Negro surgeon is visiting, pride cuts down the pain. And although the hair of the first class of colored nurses was declared unseemly for the official Bellevue nurse's cap, there are thirty-five of them now—all dedicated and superb in their profession.

Nobody says it's pretty here; nobody says it's easy either. What it is is decisive, and if you pay attention to the street plans, all laid out, the City can't hurt you.

I haven't got any muscles, so I can't really be expected to defend myself. But I do know how to take precaution. Mostly it's making sure no one knows all there is to know about me. Second, I watch everything and everyone and try to figure out their plans, their reasonings, long before they do. You have to understand what it's like, taking on a big city: I'm exposed to all sorts of ignorance and criminality. Still, this is the only life for me. I like the way the City makes people think they can do what they want and get away with it. I see them all over the place: wealthy whites, and plain ones too, pile into mansions decorated and redecorated by black women richer than they are, and both are pleased with the spectacle of the other. I've seen the eyes of black Jews, brimful of pity for everyone not themselves, graze the food stalls and the ankles of loose women, while a breeze stirs the white plumes on the helmets of the UNIA men. A colored man floats down out of the sky blowing a saxophone, and below him, in the space between two buildings, a girl talks earnestly to a man in a straw hat. He touches her lip to remove a bit of something there. Suddenly she is quiet. He tilts her chin up. They stand there. Her grip on her purse slackens and her neck makes a nice curve. The man puts his hand on the stone wall above her head. By the way his jaw moves and the turn of his head I know he has a golden tongue. The sun sneaks into the alley behind them. It makes a pretty picture on its way down.

Do what you please in the City, it is there to back and frame you no matter what you do. And what goes on on its blocks and lots and side streets is anything the strong can think of and the weak will admire. All you have to do is heed the design—the way it's laid out for you, considerate, mindful of where you want to go and what you might need tomorrow.

I lived a long time, maybe too much, in my own mind. People say I should come out more. Mix. I agree that I close off in places, but if you have been left standing, as I have, while your partner overstays at another appointment, or promises to give you exclusive attention after supper, but is falling asleep just as you have begun to speak—well, it can make you inhospitable if you aren't careful, the last thing I want to be.

Hospitality is gold in this City; you have to be clever to figure out how to be welcoming and defensive at the same time. When to love something and when to quit. If you don't know how, you can end up out of control or controlled by some outside thing like that hard case last winter. Word was that underneath the good times and the easy money something evil ran the streets and nothing was safe—not even the dead. Proof of this being Violet's outright attack on the very subject of a funeral ceremony. Barely three days into 1926. A host of thoughtful people looked at the signs (the weather, the number, their own dreams) and believed it was the commencement of all sorts of destruction. That the scandal was a message sent to warn the good and rip up the faithless. I don't know who was more ambitious—the doomsayers or Violet—but it's hard to match the superstitious for great expectations.

Armistice was seven years old the winter Violet disrupted the funeral, and veterans on Seventh Avenue were still wearing their army-issue greatcoats, because nothing they can pay for is as sturdy or hides so well what they had boasted of in 1919. Eight years later, the day before Violet's misbehavior, when the snow comes it sits where it falls on Lexington and Park Avenue too, and waits for horse-drawn wagons to tamp it down when they deliver coal for the furnaces cooling down in the cellars. Up in those big five-story apartment buildings and the narrow wooden houses in between people knock on each other's doors to see if anything is needed or can be had. A piece of soap? A little kerosene? Some fat, chicken or pork, to brace the soup one more time? Whose husband is getting ready to go see if he can find a shop open? Is there time to add turpentine to the list drawn up and handed to him by the wives?

Breathing hurts in weather that cold, but whatever the problems of being winterbound in the City they put up with them because it is worth anything to be on Lenox Avenue safe from fays and the things they think up; where the sidewalks, snow-covered or not, are wider than the main roads of the towns where they were born and perfectly ordinary people can stand at the stop, get on the streetcar, give the man the nickel, and ride anywhere you please, although you don't please to go many places because everything you want is right where you are: the church, the store, the party, the women, the men, the postbox (but no high schools), the furniture store, street newspaper vendors, the bootleg houses (but no banks), the beauty parlors, the barbershops, the juke joints, the ice wagons, the rag collectors, the pool halls, the open food markets, the number runner, and every club, organization, group, order, union, society, brotherhood, sisterhood or association imaginable. The service trails, of course, are worn, and there are paths slick from the forays of members of one group into the territory of another where it is believed something curious or thrilling lies. Some gleaming, cracking, scary stuff. Where you can pop the cork and put the cold glass mouth right up to your own. Where you can find danger or be it; where you can fight till you drop and smile at the knife when it misses and when it doesn't. It makes you wonderful just to see it. And just as wonderful to know that back in one's own building there are lists drawn up by the wives for the husband hunting an open market, and that sheets impossible to hang out in snowfall drape kitchens like the curtains of Abyssinian Sunday-school plays.

The young are not so young here, and there is no such thing as midlife. Sixty years, forty, even, is as much as anybody feels like being bothered with. If they reach that, or get very old, they sit around looking at goings-on as though it were a five-cent triple feature on Saturday. Otherwise they find themselves butting in the business of people whose names they can't even remember and whose business is none of theirs. Just to hear themselves talk and the joy of watching the distressed faces of those listening. I've known a few exceptions. Some old people who didn't slap the children for being slappable; who saved that strength in case it was needed for something important. A last courtship full of smiles and little presents. Or the dedicated care of an old friend who might not make it through without them. Sometimes they concentrated on making sure the person they had shared their long lives with had cheerful company and the necessary things for the night.

But up there on Lenox, in Violet and Joe Trace's apartment, the rooms are like the empty birdcages wrapped in cloth. And a dead girl's face has become a necessary thing for their nights. They each take turns to throw off the bedcovers, rise up from the sagging mattress and tiptoe over cold linoleum into the parlor to gaze at what seems like the only living presence in the house: the photograph of a bold, unsmiling girl staring from the mantelpiece. If the tiptoer is Joe Trace, driven by loneliness from his wife's side, then the face stares at him without hope or regret and it is the absence of accusation that wakes him from his sleep hungry for her company. No finger points. Her lips don't turn down in judgment. Her face is calm, generous and sweet. But if the tiptoer is Violet the photograph is not that at all. The girl's face looks greedy, haughty and very lazy. The cream-at-the-top-of-the-milkpail face of someone who will never work for anything; someone who picks up things lying on other people's dressers and is not embarrassed when found out. It is the face of a sneak who glides over to your sink to rinse the fork you have laid by her plate. An inward face—whatever it sees is its own self. You are there, it says, because I am looking at you.

Two or three times during the night, as they take turns to go look at that picture, one of them will say her name. Dorcas? Dorcas. The dark rooms grow darker: the parlor needs a struck match to see the face. Beyond are the dining room, two bedrooms, the kitchen—all situated in the middle of the building so the apartment's windows have no access to the moon or the light of a street lamp. The bathroom has the best light since it juts out past the kitchen and catches the afternoon rays. Violet and Joe have arranged their furnishings in a way that might not remind anybody of the rooms in *Modern Homemaker* but it suits the habits of the body, the way a person walks from one room to another without bumping into anything, and what he wants to do when he sits down. You know how some people put a chair or a table in a corner where it looks nice but nobody in the world is ever going to go over to it, let alone sit down there? Violet didn't do that in her place. Everything is put where a person would like to have it, or would use or need it. So the dining room doesn't have a dining table with funeral-parlor chairs. It has big deep-down chairs and a card table by the window covered with jade, dracena and doctor plants until they want to have card games or play tonk between themselves. The kitchen is roomy enough to accommodate four people eating or give a customer plenty legroom while Violet does her hair. The front room, or parlor, is not wasted either, waiting for a wedding reception to be worthy of. It has birdcages and mirrors for the birds to look at themselves in, but now, of course, there are no birds, Violet having let them out on the day she went to Dorcas' funeral with a knife. Now there are just empty cages, the lonely mirrors glancing back at them. As for the rest, it's a sofa, some carved wooden chairs with small tables by them so you can put your coffee cup or a dish of ice cream down in front of you, or if you want to read the paper, you can do it easy without messing up the folds. The mantel over the fireplace used to have shells and pretty-colored stones, but all of that is gone now and only the picture of Dorcas Manfred sits there in a silver frame waking them up all night long.

Such restless nights make them sleep late, and Violet has to hurry to get a meal prepared before getting ready for her round of heads. Having a knack for it, but no supervised training, and therefore no license to do it, Violet can only charge twenty-five or fifty cents anyway, but since that business at Dorcas' funeral, many of her regular customers have found reasons to do their own hair or have a daughter heat up the irons. Violet and Joe Trace didn't use to need that hairdressing pocket change, but now that Joe is skipping workdays Violet carries her tools and her trade more and more into the overheated apartments of women who wake in the afternoon, pour gin in their tea and don't care what she has done. These women always need their hair done, and sometimes pity darkens their shiny eyes and they tip her a whole dollar.

"You need to eat you something," one says to her. "Don't you want to be bigger than your curling iron?"

"Shut your mouth," says Violet.

"I mean it," says the woman. She is still sleepy, and rests her cheek in her left hand while holding her ear with the right. "Men wear you down to a sharp piece of gristle if you let them."

"Women," answers Violet. "Women wear me down. No man ever wore me down to nothing. It's these little hungry girls acting like women. Not content with boys their own age, no, they want somebody old enough to be their father. Switching round with lipstick, see-through stockings, dresses up to their you-know-what . . ."

"That's my ear, girl! You going to press it too?"

"Sorry. I'm sorry. Really, really sorry." And Violet stops to blow her nose and blot tears with the back of her hand.

"Aw, the devil," the woman sighs and takes advantage of the pause to light a cigarette. "Now I reckon you going to tell me some old hateful story about how a young girl messed over you and how *he*'s not to blame because *he* was just walking down the street minding *his* own business, when this little twat jumped on his back and dragged him off to her bed. Save your breath. You'll need it on your deathbed."

"I need my breath now." Violet tests the hot comb. It scorches a long brown finger on the newspaper.

"Did he move out? Is he with her?"

"No. We still together. She's dead."

"Dead? Then what's the matter with you?"

"He thinks about her all the time. Nothing on his mind but her. Won't work. Can't sleep. Grieves all day, all night . . ."

"Oh," says the woman. She knocks the fire from her cigarette, pinches the tip and lays the butt carefully into the ashtray. Leaning back in the chair, she presses the rim of her ear with two fingers. "You in trouble," she says, yawning. "Deep, deep trouble. Can't rival the dead for love. Lose every time."

Violet agrees that it must be so; not only is she losing Joe to a dead girl, but she wonders if she isn't falling in love with her too. When she isn't trying to humiliate Joe, she is admiring the dead girl's hair; when she isn't cursing Joe with brand-new cuss words, she is having whispered conversations with the corpse in her head; when she isn't worrying about his loss of appetite, his insomnia, she wonders what color were Dorcas' eyes. Her aunt had said brown; the beauticians said black but Violet had never seen a light-skinned person with coal-black eyes. One thing, for sure, she needed her ends cut. In the photograph and from what Violet could remember from the coffin, the girl needed her ends cut. Hair that long gets fraggely easy. Just a quarter-inch trim would do wonders, Dorcas. Dorcas.

Violet leaves the sleepy woman's house. The slush at the curb is freezing again, and although she has seven icy blocks ahead, she is grateful that the customer who is coming to her kitchen for an appointment is not due until three o'clock, and there is time for a bit of housekeeping before then. Some business that needs doing because it is impossible to have nothing to do, no sequence of errands, list of tasks. She might wave her hands in the air, or tremble if she can't put her hand to something with another chore just around the bend from the one she is doing. She lights the oven to warm up the kitchen.

And while she sprinkles the collar of a white shirt her mind is at the bottom of the bed where the leg, broken clean away from the frame, is too split to nail back. When the customer comes and Violet is sudsing the thin gray hair, murmuring "Ha mercy" at appropriate breaks in the old lady's stream of confidences, Violet is resituating the cord that holds the stove door to its hinge and rehearsing the month's plea for three more days to the rent collector. She thinks she longs for rest, a carefree afternoon to decide suddenly to go to the pictures, or just to sit with the birdcages and listen to the children play in snow.

This notion of rest, it's attractive to her, but I don't think she would like it. They are all like that, these women. Waiting for the ease, the space that need not be filled with anything other than the drift of their own thoughts. But they wouldn't like it. They are busy and thinking of ways to be busier because such a space of nothing pressing to do would knock them down. No fields of cowslips will rush into that opening, nor mornings free of flies and heat when the light is shy. No. Not at all. They fill their mind and hands with soap and repair and dicey confrontations because what is waiting for them, in a suddenly idle moment, is the seep of rage. Molten. Thick and slow-moving. Mindful and particular about what in its path it chooses to bury. Or else, into a beat of time, and sideways under their breasts, slips a sorrow they don't know where from. A neighbor returns the spool of thread she borrowed, and not just the thread, but the extra-long needle too, and both of them stand in the door frame a moment while the borrower repeats for the lender a funny conversation she had with the woman on the floor below; it *is* funny and they laugh—one loudly while holding her forehead, the other hard enough to hurt her stomach. The lender closes the door, and later, still smiling, touches the lapel of her sweater to her eye to wipe traces of the laughter away then drops to the arm of the sofa the tears coming so fast she needs two hands to catch them.

So Violet sprinkles the collars and cuffs. Then sudses with all her heart those three or four ounces of gray hair, soft and interesting as a baby's.

Not the kind of baby hair her grandmother had soaped and played with and remembered for forty years. The hair of the little boy who got his name from it. Maybe that is why Violet is a hairdresser—all those years of listening to her rescuing grandmother, True Belle, tell Baltimore stories. The years with Miss Vera Louise in the fine stone house on Edison Street, where the linen was embroidered with blue thread and there was nothing to do but raise and adore the blond boy who ran away from them depriving everybody of his carefully loved hair.

Folks were furious when Violet broke up the funeral, but I can't believe they were surprised. Way, way before that, before Joe ever laid eyes on the girl, Violet sat down in the middle of the street. She didn't stumble nor was she pushed: she just sat down. After a few minutes two men and a woman came to her, but she couldn't make out why or what they said. Someone tried to give her water to drink, but she knocked it away. A policeman knelt in front of her and she rolled over on her side, covering her eyes. He would have taken her in but for the assembling crowd murmuring, "Aw, she's tired. Let her rest." They carried her to the nearest steps. Slowly she came around, dusted off her clothes, and got to her appointment an hour late, which pleased the slow-moving whores, who never hurried anything but love.

It never happened again as far as I know—the street sitting—but quiet as it's kept she did try to steal that baby although there is no way to prove it. What is known is this: the

Dumfrey women—mother and daughter—weren't home when Violet arrived. Either they got the date mixed up or had decided to go to a legally licensed parlor—just for the shampoo, probably, because there is no way to get that deepdown hair washing at a bathroom sink. The beauticians have it beat when it comes to that: you get to lie back instead of lean forward; you don't have to press a towel in your eyes to keep the soapy water out because at a proper beauty parlor it drains down the back of your head into the sink. So, sometimes, even if the legal beautician is not as adept as Violet, a regular customer will sneak to a shop just for the pleasure of a comfy shampoo.

Doing two heads in one place was lucky and Violet looked forward to the eleven-o'clock appointment. When nobody answered the bell, she waited, thinking maybe they'd been held up at the market. She tried the bell again, after some time, and then leaned over the concrete banister to ask a woman leaving the building next door if she knew where the Dumfrey women were. The woman shook her head but came over to help Violet look at the windows and wonder.

"They keep the shades up when they home," she said. "Down when they gone. Should be just the reverse."

"Maybe they want to see out when they home," said Violet.

"See what?" asked the woman. She was instantly angry.

"Daylight," said Violet. "Have some daylight get in there."

"They need to move on back to Memphis then if daylight is what they want."

"Memphis? I thought they were born here."

"That's what they'd have you believe. But they ain't. Not even Memphis. Cottown. Someplace nobody ever heard of."

"I'll be," said Violet. She was very surprised because the Dumfrey women were graceful, citified ladies whose father owned a store on 136th Street, and themselves had nice paper-handling jobs: one took tickets at the Lafayette; the other worked in the counting house.

"They don't like it known," the woman went on.

"Why?" asked Violet.

"Hincty, that's why. Comes from handling money all day. You notice that? How people who handle money for a living get stuck-up? Like it was theirs instead of yours?" She sucked her teeth at the shaded windows. "Daylight my foot."

"Well, I do their hair every other Tuesday and today is Tuesday, right?"

"All day."

"Wonder where they are, then?"

The woman slipped a hand under her skirt to reknot the top of her stocking. "Off somewhere trying to sound like they ain't from Cottown."

"Where you from?" Violet was impressed with the woman's ability to secure her hose with one hand.

"Cottown. Knew both of them from way back. Come up here, the whole family act like they never set eyes on me before. Comes from handling money instead of a broom which I better get to before I lose this no-count job. O Jesus." She sighed heavily. "Leave a note, why don't you? Don't count on me to let them know you was here. We don't speak if we don't have to." She buttoned her coat, then moved her hand in a suit-yourself wave when Violet said she'd wait a bit longer.

Violet sat down on the wide steps nestling her bag of irons and oil and shampoo in the space behind her calves.

When the baby was in her arms, she inched its blanket up around the cheeks against the threat of wind too cool for its honey-sweet, butter-colored face. Its big-eyed noncommittal stare made her smile. Comfort settled itself in her stomach and a kind of skipping, running light traveled her veins.

Joe will love this, she thought. Love it. And quickly her mind raced ahead to their bedroom and what was in there she could use for a crib until she got a real one. There was gentle soap in the sample case already so she could bathe him in the kitchen right away. Him? Was it a him? Violet lifted her head to the sky and laughed with the excitement in store when she got home to look. It was the laugh—loose and loud—that confirmed the theft for some and discredited it for others. Would a sneak-thief woman stealing a baby call attention to herself like that at a corner not a hundred yards away from the wicker carriage she took it from? Would a kindhearted innocent woman take a stroll with an infant she was asked to watch while its older sister ran back in the house, and laugh like that?

The sister was screaming in front of her house, drawing neighbors and passersby to her as she scanned the sidewalk—up and down—shouting "Philly! Philly's gone! She took Philly!" She kept her hands on the baby buggy's push bar, unwilling to run whichever way her gaze landed, as though, if she left the carriage, empty except for the record she dropped in it—the one she had dashed back into the house for and that was now on the pillow where her baby brother used to be—maybe it too would disappear.

"She who?" somebody asked. "Who took him?"

"A woman! I was gone one minute. Not even one! I asked her . . . I said . . . and she said okay . . . !"

"You left a whole live baby with a stranger to go get a record?" The disgust in the man's voice brought tears to the girl's eyes. "I hope your mama tears you up and down."

Opinions, decisions popped through the crowd like struck matches.

"Ain't got the sense of a gnat."

"Who misraised you?"

"Call the cops."

"What for?"

"They can at least look."

"Will you just look at what she left that baby for."

"What is it?"

" 'The Trombone Blues.' "

"Have mercy."

"She'll know more about blues than any trombone when her mama gets home."

The little knot of people, more and more furious at the stupid, irresponsible sister, at the cops, at the record lying where a baby should be, had just about forgotten the kidnapper when a man at the curb said, "That her?" He pointed to Violet at the corner and it was when everybody turned toward where his finger led that Violet, tickled by the pleasure of discovery she was soon to have, threw back her head and laughed out loud.

The proof of her innocence lay in the bag of hairdressing utensils, which remained on the steps where Violet had been waiting.

"Would I leave my bag, with the stuff I make my living with if I was stealing your baby? You think I'm crazy?" Violet's eyes, squinted and smoking with fury, stared right at the sister. "In fact, I would have taken everything. Buggy too, if that's what I was doing."

It sounded true and likely to most of the crowd, especially those who faulted the sister. The woman had left her bag and was merely walking the baby while the older sister—too silly to be minding a child anyway—ran back in her house for a record to play for a friend. And who knew what else was going on in the head of a girl too dumb to watch a baby sleep?

It sounded unlikely and mighty suspicious to a minority.

Why would she walk that far, if she was just playing, rocking the baby? Why not pace in front of the house like normal? And what kind of laugh was that? What kind? If she could laugh like that, she could forget not only her bag but the whole world.

The sister, chastised, took baby, buggy, and "Trombone Blues" back up the steps.

Violet, triumphant and angry, snatched her bag, saying, "Last time I do anybody a favor on this block. Watch your own damn babies!" And she thought of it that way ever after, remembering the incident as an outrage to her character. The makeshift crib, the gentle soap left her mind. The memory of the light, however, that had skipped through her veins came back now and then, and once in a while, on an overcast day, when certain corners in the room resisted lamplight; when the red beans in the pot seemed to be taking forever to soften, she imagined a brightness that could be carried in her arms. Distributed, if need be, into places dark as the bottom of a well.

Joe never learned of Violet's public crazinesses. Stuck, Gistan and other male friends passed word of the incidents to each other, but couldn't bring themselves to say much more to him than "How *is* Violet? Doing okay, is she?" Her private cracks, however, were known to him.

I call them cracks because that is what they were. Not openings or breaks, but dark fissures in the globe light of the day. She wakes up in the morning and sees with perfect clarity a string of small, well-lit scenes. In each one something specific is being done: food things, work things; customers and acquaintances are encountered, places entered. But she does not see herself doing these things. She sees them being done. The globe light holds and bathes each scene, and it can be assumed that at the curve where the light stops is a solid foundation. In truth, there is no foundation at all, but alleyways, crevices one steps across all the time. But the globe light is imperfect too. Closely examined it shows seams, ill-glued cracks and weak places beyond which is anything. Anything at all. Sometimes when Violet isn't paying attention she stumbles onto these cracks, like the time when, instead of putting her left heel forward, she stepped back and folded her legs in order to sit in the street.

She didn't use to be that way. She had been a snappy, determined girl and a hardworking young woman, with the snatch-gossip tongue of a beautician. She liked, and had, to get her way. She had chosen Joe and refused to go back home once she'd seen him taking shape in early light. She had butted their way out of the Tenderloin district into a spacious uptown apartment promised to another family by sitting out the landlord, haunting his doorway. She collected customers by going up to them and describing her services ("I can do your hair better and cheaper, and do it when and where you want"). She argued butchers and wagon vendors into prime and extra ("Put that little end piece in. You weighing the stalks; I'm buying the leaf"). Long before Joe stood in the drugstore watching a girl buy candy, Violet had stumbled into a crack or two. Felt the anything-at-all begin in her mouth. Words connected only to themselves pierced an otherwise normal comment.

"I don't believe an eight has been out this month," she says, thinking about the daily number combinations. "Not one. Bound to come up soon, so I'm hanging an eight on everything."

"That's no way to play," says Joe. "Get you a combo and stay with it."

"No. Eight is due, I know it. Was all over the place in August—all summer, in fact. Now it's ready to come out of hiding."

"Suit yourself." Joe is examining a shipment of Cleopatra products.

"Got a mind to double it with an aught and two or three others just in case who is that pretty girl standing next to you?" She looks up at Joe expecting an answer.

"What?" He frowns. "What you say?"

"Oh." Violet blinks rapidly. "Nothing. I mean . . . nothing."

"Pretty girl?"

"Nothing, Joe. Nothing."

She means nothing can be done about it, but it was something. Something slight, but troublesome. Like the time Miss Haywood asked her what time could she do her granddaughter's hair and Violet said, "Two o'clock if the hearse is out of the way."

Extricating herself from these collapses is not too hard, because nobody presses her. Did they do the same? Maybe. Maybe everybody has a renegade tongue yearning to be on its own. Violet shuts up. Speaks less and less until "uh" or "have mercy" carry almost all of her part of a conversation. Less excusable than a wayward mouth is an independent hand that can find in a parrot's cage a knife lost for weeks. Violet is still as well as silent. Over time her silences annoy her husband, then puzzle him and finally depress him. He is married to a woman who speaks mainly to her birds. One of whom answers back: "I love you."

Or used to. When Violet threw out the birds, it left her not only without the canaries' company and the parrot's confession but also minus the routine of covering their cages, a habit that had become one of those necessary things for the night. The things that help you sleep all the way through it. Back-breaking labor might do it; or liquor. Surely a body—friendly if not familiar—lying next to you. Someone whose touch is a reassurance, not an affront or a nuisance. Whose heavy breathing neither enrages nor disgusts, but amuses you like that of a cherished pet. And rituals help too: door locking, tidying up, cleaning teeth, arranging hair, but they are preliminaries to the truly necessary things. Most people want to crash into sleep. Get knocked into it with a fist of fatigue to avoid a night of noisy silence, empty birdcages that don't need wrapping in cloth, of bold unsmiling girls staring from the mantelpiece.

For Violet, who never knew the girl, only her picture and the personality she invented for her based on careful investigations, the girl's memory is a sickness in the house—everywhere and nowhere. There is nothing for Violet to beat or hit and when she has to, just has to strike it somehow, there is nothing left but straw or a sepia print.

But for Joe it is different. That girl had been his necessary thing for three months of nights. He remembers his memories of her; how thinking about her as he lay in bed next to Violet was the way he entered sleep. He minds her death, is so sorry about it, but minded more the possibility of his memory failing to conjure up the dearness. And he knows it will continue to fade because it was already beginning to the afternoon he hunted Dorcas down. After she said she wanted Coney Island and rent parties and more of Mexico. Even then he was clinging to the quality of her sugar-flawed skin, the high wild bush the bed pillows made of her hair, her bitten nails, the heartbreaking way she stood, toes pointed in. Even then, listening to her talk, to the terrible things she said, he felt he was losing the timbre of her voice and what happened to her eyelids when they made love.

Now he lies in bed remembering every detail of that October afternoon when he first met her, from start to finish, and over and over. Not just because it is tasty, but because he is trying to sear her into his mind, brand her there against future wear.

So that neither she nor the alive love of her will fade or scab over the way it had with Violet. For when Joe tries to remember the way it was when he and Violet were young, when they got married, decided to leave Vesper County and move up North to the City almost nothing comes to mind. He recalls dates, of course, events, purchases, activity, even scenes. But he has a tough time trying to catch what it felt like.

He had struggled a long time with that loss, believed he had resigned himself to it, had come to terms with the fact that old age would be not remembering what things felt like. That you could say, "I was scared to death," but you could not retrieve the fear. That you could replay in the brain the scene of ecstasy, of murder, of tenderness, but it was drained of everything but the language to say it in. He thought he had come to terms with that but he had been wrong. When he called on Sheila to deliver her Cleopatra order, he entered a roomful of laughing, teasing women—and there she was, standing at the door, holding it open for him—the same girl that had distracted him in the drugstore; the girl buying candy and ruining her skin had moved him so his eyes burned. Then, suddenly, there in Alice Manfred's doorway, she stood, toes pointing in, hair braided, not even smiling but welcoming him in for sure. For sure. Otherwise he would not have had the audacity, the nerve, to whisper to her at the door as he left.

It was a randy aggressiveness he had enjoyed because he had not used or needed it before. The ping of desire that surfaced along with his whisper through the closing door he began to curry. First he pocketed it, taking pleasure in knowing it was there. Then he unboxed it to bring out and admire at his leisure. He did not yearn or pine for the girl, rather he thought about her, and decided. Just as he had decided on his name, the walnut tree he and Victory slept in, a piece of bottomland, and when to head for the City, he decided on Dorcas. Regarding his marriage to Violet—he had not chosen that but was grateful, in fact, that he didn't have to; that Violet did it for him, helping him escape all the redwings in the county and the ripe silence that accompanied them.

They met in Vesper County, Virginia, under a walnut tree. She had been working in the fields like everybody else, and stayed past picking time to live with a family twenty miles away from her own. They knew people in common; and suspected they had at least one relative in common. They were drawn together because they had been put together, and all they decided for themselves was when and where to meet at night.

Violet and Joe left Tyrell, a railway stop through Vesper County, in 1906, and boarded the colored section of the Southern Sky. When the train trembled approaching the water surrounding the City, they thought it was like them: nervous at having gotten there at last, but terrified of what was on the other side. Eager, a little scared, they did not even nap during the fourteen hours of a ride smoother than a rocking cradle. The quick darkness in the carriage cars when they shot through a tunnel made them wonder if maybe there was a wall ahead to crash into or a cliff hanging over nothing. The train shivered with them at the thought but went on and sure enough there was ground up ahead and the trembling became the dancing under their feet. Joe stood up, his fingers clutching the baggage rack above his head. He felt the dancing better that way, and told Violet to do the same.

They were hanging there, a young country couple, laughing and tapping back at the tracks, when the attendant came through, pleasant but unsmiling now that he didn't have to smile in this car full of colored people.

"Breakfast in the dining car. Breakfast in the dining car. Good morning. Full breakfast in the dining car." He held a carriage blanket over his arm and from underneath it drew a pint bottle of milk, which he placed in the hands of a young woman with a baby asleep across her knees. "Full breakfast."

He never got his way, this attendant. He wanted the whole coach to file into the dining car, now that they could. Immediately, now that they were out of Delaware and a long way from Maryland there would be no green-as-poison curtain separating the colored people eating from the rest of the diners. The cooks would not feel obliged to pile extra helpings on the plates headed for the curtain; three lemon slices in the iced tea, two pieces of coconut cake arranged to look like one—to take the sting out of the curtain; homey it up with a little extra on the plate. Now, skirting the City, there were no green curtains; the whole car could be full of colored people and everybody on a first-come first-serve basis. If only they would. If only they would tuck those little boxes and baskets underneath the seat; close those paper bags, for once, put the bacon-stuffed biscuits back into the cloth they were wrapped in, and troop single file through the five cars ahead on into the dining car, where the table linen was at least as white as the sheets they dried on juniper bushes; where the napkins were folded with a crease as stiff as the ones they ironed for Sunday dinner; where the gravy was as smooth as their own, and the biscuits did not take second place to the bacon-stuffed ones they wrapped in cloth. Once in a while it happened. Some well-shod woman with two young girls, a preacherly kind of man with a watch chain and a rolled-brim hat might stand up, adjust their clothes and weave through the coaches toward the tables, foamy white with heavy silvery knives and forks. Presided over and waited upon by a black man who did not have to lace his dignity with a smile.

Joe and Violet wouldn't think of it—paying money for a meal they had not missed and that required them to sit still at, or worse, separated by, a table. Not now. Not entering the lip of the City dancing all the way. Her hip bones rubbed his thigh as they stood in the aisle unable to stop smiling. They weren't even there yet and already the City was speaking to them. They were dancing. And like a million others, chests pounding, tracks controlling their feet, they stared out the windows for first sight of the City that danced with them, proving already how much it loved them. Like a million more they could hardly wait to get there and love it back.

Some were slow about it and traveled from Georgia to Illinois, to the City, back to Georgia, out to San Diego and finally, shaking their heads, surrendered themselves to the City. Others knew right away that it was for them, this City and no other. They came on a whim because there it was and why not? They came after much planning, many letters written to and from, to make sure and know how and how much and where. They came for a visit and forgot to go back to tall cotton or short. Discharged with or without honor, fired with or without severance, dispossessed with or without notice, they hung around for a while and then could not imagine themselves anywhere else. Others came because a relative or hometown buddy said, Man, you best see this place before you die; or, We got room now, so pack your suitcase and don't bring no high-top shoes.

However they came, when or why, the minute the leather of their soles hit the pavement—there was no turning around. Even if the room they rented was smaller than the heifer's stall and darker than a morning privy, they stayed to look at their number, hear themselves in an audience, feel themselves moving down the street among hundreds of others who moved the way they did, and who, when they spoke, regardless of the accent, treated language like the same intricate, malleable toy designed for their play. Part of why they loved it was the specter they left behind. The slumped spines of the veterans of the 27th Battalion betrayed by the commander for whom they had fought like lunatics. The eyes of thousands, stupefied with disgust at having been imported by Mr. Armour, Mr. Swift, Mr. Montgomery Ward to break strikes then dismissed for having done so. The broken shoes of two thousand Galveston longshoremen that Mr. Mallory would never pay fifty cents an hour like the white ones. The praying palms, the raspy breathing, the quiet children of the ones who had escaped from Springfield Ohio, Springfield Indiana, Greensburg Indiana, Wilmington Delaware, New Orleans Louisiana, after raving whites had foamed all over the lanes and yards of home.

The wave of black people running from want and violence crested in the 1870s; the '80s; the '90s but was a steady stream in 1906 when Joe and Violet joined it. Like the others, they were country people, but how soon country people forget. When they fall in love with a city, it is for forever, and it is like forever. As though there never was a time when they didn't love it. The minute they arrive at the train station or get off the ferry and glimpse the wide streets and the wasteful lamps lighting them, they know they are born for it. There, in a city, they are not so much new as themselves: their stronger, riskier selves. And in the beginning when they first arrive, and twenty years later when they and the City have grown up, they love that part of themselves so much they forget what loving other people was like—if they ever knew, that is. I don't mean they hate them, no, just that what they start to love is the way a person is in the City; the way a schoolgirl never pauses at a stoplight but looks up and down the street before stepping off the curb; how men accommodate themselves to tall buildings and wee porches, what a woman looks like moving in a crowd, or how shocking her profile is against the backdrop of the East River. The restfulness in kitchen chores when she knows the lamp oil or the staple is just around the corner and not seven miles away; the amazement of throwing open the window and being hypnotized for hours by people on the street below.

Little of that makes for love, but it does pump desire. The woman who churned a man's blood as she leaned all alone on a fence by a country road might not expect even to catch his eye in the City. But if she is clipping quickly down the big-city street in heels, swinging her purse, or sitting on a stoop with a cool beer in her hand, dangling her shoe from the toes of her foot, the man, reacting to her posture, to soft skin on stone, the weight of the building stressing the delicate, dangling shoe, is captured. And he'd think it was the woman he wanted, and not some combination of curved stone, and a swinging, high-heeled shoe moving in and out of sunlight. He would know right away the deception, the trick of shapes and light and movement, but it wouldn't matter at all because the deception was part of it too. Anyway, he could feel his lungs going in and out. There is no air in the City but there is breath, and every morning it races through him like laughing gas brightening his eyes, his talk, and his expectations. In no time at all he forgets little pebbly creeks and apple trees so old they lay their branches along the ground and you have to reach down or stoop to pick the fruit. He forgets a sun that used to slide up like the yolk of a good country egg, thick and red-orange at the bottom of the sky, and he doesn't miss it, doesn't look up to see what happened to it or to stars made irrelevant by the light of thrilling, wasteful street lamps.

That kind of fascination, permanent and out of control, seizes children, young girls, men of every description, mothers, brides, and barfly women, and if they have their way and get to the City, they feel more like themselves, more like the people they always believed they were. Nothing can pry them away from that; the City is what they want it to be: thriftless, warm, scary and full of amiable strangers. No wonder they forget pebbly creeks and when they do not forget the sky completely think of it as a tiny piece of information about the time of day or night.

But I have seen the City do an unbelievable sky. Redcaps and dining-car attendants who wouldn't think of moving out of the City sometimes go on at great length about country skies they have seen from the windows of trains. But there is nothing to beat what the City can make of a nightsky. It can empty itself of surface, and more like the ocean than the ocean itself, go deep, starless. Close up on the tops of buildings, near, nearer than the cap you are wearing, such a citysky presses and retreats, presses and retreats, making me think of the free but illegal love of sweethearts before they are discovered. Looking at it, this nightsky booming over a glittering city, it's possible for me to avoid dreaming of what I know is in the ocean, and the bays and tributaries it feeds: the two-seat aeroplanes, nose down in the muck, pilot and passenger staring at schools of passing bluefish; money, soaked and salty in canvas bags, or waving their edges gently from metal bands made to hold them forever. They are down there, along with yellow flowers that eat water beetles and eggs floating away from thrashing fins; along with the children who made a mistake in the parents they chose; along with slabs of Carrara pried from unfashionable buildings. There are bottles too, made of glass beautiful enough to rival stars I cannot see above me because the citysky has hidden them. Otherwise, if it wanted to, it could show me stars cut from the lamé gowns of chorus girls, or mirrored in the eyes of sweethearts furtive and happy under the pressure of a deep, touchable sky.

But that's not all a citysky can do. It can go purple and keep an orange heart so the clothes of the people on the streets glow like dance-hall costumes. I have seen women stir shirts into boiled starch or put the tiniest stitches into their hose while a girl straightens the hair of her sister at the stove, and all the while heaven, unnoticed and as beautiful as an Iroquois, drifts past their windows. As well as the windows where sweethearts, free and illegal, tell each other things.

Twenty years after Joe and Violet train-danced on into the City, they were still a couple but barely speaking to each other, let alone laughing together or acting like the ground was a dance-hall floor. Convinced that he alone remembers those days, and wants them back, aware of what it looked like but not at all of what it felt like, he coupled himself elsewhere. He rented a room from a neighbor who knows the exact cost of her discretion. Six hours a week he has purchased. Time for the citysky to move from a thin ice blue to purple with a heart of gold. And time enough, when the sun sinks, to tell his new love things he never told his wife.

Important things like how the hibiscus smells on the bank of a stream at dusk; how he can barely see his knees poking through the holes in his trousers in that light, so what makes him think he can see her hand even if she did decide to shove it through the bushes and confirm, for once and for all, that she was indeed his mother? And even though the confirmation would shame him, it would make him the happiest boy in Virginia. If she decided, that is, to show him it, to listen for once to what he was saying to her and then do it, say some kind of yes, even if it was no, so he would know. And how he was willing to take that chance of being humiliated and grateful at the same time, because the confirmation would mean both. Her hand, her fingers poking through the blossoms, touching his; maybe letting him touch hers. He wouldn't have grabbed it, snatched it and dragged her out from behind the bushes. Maybe that's what she was afraid of, but he wouldn't have done that, and he told her so. Just a sign, he said, just show me your hand, he said, and I'll know don't you know I have to know? She wouldn't have to say anything, although nobody had ever heard her say anything; it wouldn't have to be words; he didn't need words or even want them because he knew how they could lie, could heat your blood and disappear. She wouldn't even have to say the word "mother." Nothing like that. All she had to do was give him a sign, her hand thrust through the leaves, the white flowers, would be enough to say that she knew him to be the one, the son she had fourteen years ago, and ran away from, but not too far. Just far enough away to annoy everybody because she was not completely gone, and close enough to scare everybody because she creeps about and hides and touches and laughs a low sweet babygirl laugh in the cane.

Maybe she did it. Maybe those were her fingers moving like that in the bush, not twigs, but in light so small he could not see his knees poking through the holes in his trousers, maybe he missed the sign that would have been some combination of shame and pleasure, at least, and not the inside nothing he traveled with from then on, except for the fall of 1925 when he had somebody to tell it to. Somebody called Dorcas with hooves tracing her cheekbones and who knew better than people his own age what that inside nothing was like. And who filled it for him, just as he filled it for her, because she had it too.

Maybe her nothing was worse since she knew her mother, and had even been slapped in the face by her for some sass she could not remember. But she did remember, and told him so, about the slap across her face, the pop and sting of it and how it burned. How it burned, she told him. And of all the slaps she got, that one was the one she remembered best because it was the last. She leaned out the window of her best girlfriend's house because the shouts were not part of what she was dreaming. They were outside her head, across the street. Like the running. Everybody running. For water? Buckets? The fire engine, polished and poised in another part of town? There was no getting in that house where her clothespin dolls lay in a row. In a cigar box. But she tried anyway to get them. Barefoot, in the dress she had slept in, she ran to get them, and yelled to her mother that the box of dolls, the box of dolls was up there on the dresser can we get them? Mama?

She cries again and Joe holds her close. The Iroquois sky passes the windows, and if they do see it, it crayon-colors their love. That would be when, after a decent silence, he would lift his sample case of Cleopatra from the chair and tease her before opening it, holding up the lid so she could not see right away what he has hidden under the jars and perfume-sweet boxes; the present he has brought for her. That is the little bow that ties up their day at the same time the citysky is changing its orange heart to black in order to hide its stars for the longest time before passing them out one by one by one, like gifts.

By that time she has pushed back his cuticles, cleaned his nails and painted them with clear polish. She has cried a little talking about East St. Louis, and cheers herself up with his fingernails. She likes to know that the hands lifting and turning her under the blanket have been done by her. Lotioned by her with cream from a jar of something from his sample case. She rears up and, taking his face in her hands, kisses the lids of each of his two-color eyes. One for me, she says, and one for you. One for me and one for you. Gimme this, I give you that. Gimme this. Gimme this.

They try not to shout, but can't help it. Sometimes he covers her mouth with the palm of his hand so no one passing in the hall will hear her, and if he can, if he thinks of it in time, he bites the pillow to stop his own yell. If he can. Sometimes he thinks he has stopped it, because the corner of the pillow is in his mouth all right, and then he hears himself breathing in and out, in and out, at the tail end of a shout that could only have come from his weary throat.

She laughs at that, laughs and laughs before she straddles his back to pound it with her fists. Then when she is exhausted and he half asleep, she leans down, her lips behind his ear, and makes plans. Mexico, she whispers. I want you to take me to Mexico. Too loud, he murmurs. No, no, she says, it's just right. How you know? he demands. I heard people say, people say the tables are round and have white cloths over them and wee baby lampshades. It don't open till way past your bedtime, he says smiling. This my bedtime, she says, Mexico people sleep in the day, take me. They're in there till church time Sunday morning and no whitepeople can get in, and the boys who play sometimes get up and dance with you. Uh oh, he says. What uh oh, she asks. I just want to dance with you and then go sit at a round table with a lamp on it. People can see us, he says, those little lamps you talking about big enough to show who's there.

You always say that, she giggles, like last time and nobody even looked at us they were having such a good time and Mexico is better even because nobody can see under the tablecloth, can they? Can they? If you don't want to dance, we can just sit there at the table, looking siditty by the lamplight and listen to the music and watch the people. Nobody can see under the tablecloth. Joe, Joe, take me, say you'll take me. How you going to get out the house? he asks. I'll figure it, she croons, just like always, just say yes. Well, he says, well, no point in picking the apple if you don't want to see how it taste. How does it taste, Joe? she asks. And he opens his eyes.

The door is locked and Malvonne will not be back from her 40th Street offices until way after midnight, a thought that excites them: that if it were possible they could almost spend the night together. If Alice Manfred or Violet took a trip, say, then the two of them could postpone the gift he gives her on into the darkest part of night until, smelling of Oxydol and paste wax, Malvonne came back from her offices. As it is, having made their plans for Mexico, Dorcas tips out the door and down the steps before Violet has finished her evening heads and come home around seven to find that Joe has already changed the birds' water and covered their cages. On those nights Joe does not mind lying awake next to his silent wife because his thoughts are with this young good God young girl who both blesses his life and makes him wish he had never been born.

Malvonne lived alone with newspapers and other people's stories printed in small books. When she was not making her office building sparkle, she was melding the print stories with her keen observation of the people around her. Very little escaped this woman who rode the trolley against traffic at 6:00 p.m.; who examined the trash baskets of powerful whitemen, looked at photographs of women and children on their desks. Heard their hallway conversation, and the bathroom laughter penetrating the broom closet like fumes from her bottle of ammonia. She examined their bottles and resituated the flasks tucked under cushions and behind books whose words were printed in two columns. She knew who had a passion for justice as well as ladies' undergarments, who loved his wife and who shared one. The one who fought with his son and would not speak to his father. For they did not cover the mouthpiece when they talked on the telephone to ask her to leave as she inched her way down the halls, into their offices, nor did they drop their voices to confidential whispers when they worked late doing what they called the "real" business.

But Malvonne was not interested in them; she simply noticed. Her interest lay in the neighborhood people.

Before Sweetness changed his name from William Younger to Little Caesar, he robbed a mailbox on 130th Street. Looking for postal notes, cash or what, Malvonne couldn't imagine. She had raised him from the time he was seven and a better-behaved nephew no one could have wished for. In the daytime, anyway. But some of the things he got into during Malvonne's office shift from 6:00 to 2:30 a.m. she would never know; others she learned after he left for Chicago, or was it San Diego, or some other city ending with O.

One of the things she learned explained where her grocery bag had gone—the twenty-pound salt sack she carried, nicely laundered and folded in her purse, to market. When she found it, behind the radiator in Sweetness' room, it was full of uncanceled letters. As she examined them her first impulse was to try to reseal and refold their contents and get them quickly into a mailbox. She ended, however, by reading each one including those Sweetness had not bothered to tear open. Except for the pleasure of recognizing the signatures, the reading turned out to be flatly uninteresting.

Dear Helen Moore: questions about Helen's health; answers about the writer's own. weather. deceptions. promises. love and then the signer, as though Helen received so much mail, had so many relatives and friends she couldn't remember them all, identified her or him self in large, slanting script your devoted sister, Mrs. something something; or your loving father in New York, L. Henderson Woodward.

A few of them required action on Malvonne's part. A vocational school student had sent a matchbook application to a correspondence law school along with the required, but now missing, dollar bill. Malvonne didn't have a dollar to spare for Lila Spencer's entrance fee, but she did worry that if the girl did not get to be a lawyer she would end up with an apron job. So she added a note in her own hand, saying, "I do not have the one dollar right this minute, but as soon as I hear that you received this application and agreed that I should come, I will have it by then if you tell me you don't have it and really need it."

The sad moment came when she read the letter to Panama from Winsome Clark complaining to her husband who worked in the Canal Zone about the paltriness and insufficiency of the money he had sent her—money of so little help she was giving up her job, picking up the children and returning to Barbados. Malvonne could feel the wall of life pressed up against the woman's palms; feel her hands bashed tender from pounding it; her hips constrained by the clutch of small children. "I don't know what to do," she wrote. "Nothing I do make a difference. Auntie make a racket about everything. I am besides myself. The children is miserable as me. the money you senting can not keeping all us afloat. Us drowning here and may as well drown at home where your mother is and mine and big trees."

Oh, thought Malvonne, she dreams of big trees in Barbados? Bigger than those in the park? Must be jungle for sure.

Winsome said she was "sorry your good friend dead in the big fire and pray for he and you how come so much colored people dying where whites doing great stuff. I guess you thinking that aint no grown person question. Send anything else you get to Wyndham Road where I and babies be two pay envelopes from now. Sonny say he have shoe shining money for his own passage so dont worry none except to stay among the quick. your dearest wife Mrs. Winsome Clark."

Malvonne didn't know Winsome or anybody on the 300 block of Edgecombe Avenue, although one building there was full of rich West Indians who kept pretty much to themselves and from whose windows came the odor of seasonings she didn't recognize. The point now was to get Winsome's notice of departure, already two pay envelopes ago, to Panama before any more cash went to Edgecombe where the aunt might get hold of it, and who knows, if she was as hateful as Winsome told it (watering down the children's milk on the sly and whipping the five-year-old for mishandling the hot, heavy pressing iron) she might keep the money for herself. Malvonne resealed the letter carefully and thought she would add another penny stamp in case that would help get it to Panama faster.

There was only one letter to sweat over and to wonder about

the woman who could write down such words, let alone do what she had done and promised more of. The writer lived in the same building as her lover. Malvonne did not know what made her waste a three-cent stamp other than the pleasure of knowing the government was delivering her heat. Perspiring and breathing lightly, Malvonne forced herself to read the letter several times. The problem was whether to send on to Mr. M. Sage (that was what he was called on the envelope; on the sheet of tablet paper he was called "daddy") his letter from "your always Hot Steam." A month had passed since it was written and Steam might be wondering if she had gone too far. Or had Daddy Sage and Steam done more of those lowdown sticky things in the meantime? Finally she decided to mail it with a note of her own attached—urging caution and directing daddy's attention to a clipping from *Opportunity Magazine.*

It was while she was preparing this anonymous advice that Joe Trace knocked on her door.

"How you doing, Malvonne?"

"Not complaining. How about you?"

"Can I step in? Got a proposition for you." He smiled his easy, country smile.

"I don't have a nickel, Joe."

"No." He held up his hand and walked past her into the living room. "I'm not selling. See? I don't even have my case with me."

"Oh, well, then." Malvonne followed him to the sofa. "Have a seat."

"But if I was," he said, "what would you like? If you had a nickel, I mean."

"That purple soap was kind of nice."

"You got it!"

"Went in a flash, though," said Malvonne.

"Fancy soap is fancy. Not meant to last."

"Guess not."

"I got two left. I'll bring them up right away."

"What brings this on? You ain't selling you giving away free for what reason?" Malvonne looked at the clock on the mantel, figuring out how much time she had to talk to Joe and get her letters mailed before leaving for work.

"A favor you might say."

"Or I might not say?"

"You will. It's a favor to me, but a little pocket change for you."

Malvonne laughed. "Out with it, Joe. This something Violet ain't in on?"

"Well. She. This is. Vi is. I'm not going to disturb her with this, you know?"

"No. Tell me."

"Well. I'd like to rent your place."

"What?"

"Just a afternoon or two, every now and then. While you at work. But I'll pay for the whole month."

"What you up to, Joe? You know I work at night." Maybe it was a trick name and a trick address, and Joe was "Daddy" picking up mail somewhere else and telling Steam his name was Sage.

"I know your shift's at night, but you leave at four."

"If it's nice enough to walk I do. Most time I catch the five-thirty."

"It wouldn't be every day, Malvonne."

"It wouldn't be no day. I don't think I like what you proposing."

"Two dollars each and every month."

"You think I need your money or your flimsy soap?"

"No, no, Malvonne. Look. Let me explain. Ain't many women like you understand the problems men have with their wives."

"What kind of problem?"

"Well. Violet. You know how funny she been since her Change."

"Violet funny way before that. Funny in 1920 as I recall."

"Yeah, well. But now—"

"Joe, you want to rent Sweetness' room to bring another woman in here while I'm gone just cause Violet don't want no part of you. What kind a person you think I am? Okay there's no love lost between Violet and me, but I take her part, not yours, you old dog."

"Listen here, Malvonne—"

"Who is she?"

"Nobody. I mean, I don't know yet. I just thought—"

"Ha. If you lucked up on some fool you'd have a place? That's what you thought?"

"Sort of. I may not ever use it. But I'd like it in case. I'd pay the money whether I used it or not."

"Fifty cents in certain houses get you the woman, the floor, the walls *and* the bed. Two dollars get you a woman on a store-bought scooter if you want it."

"Aw, no, Malvonne. No. You got me all wrong. I don't want nobody off the street. Good Lord."

"No? Who do you think but a streetwalker go traipsing off with you?"

"Malvonne, I'm just hoping for a lady friend. Somebody to talk to."

"Up over Violet's head? Why you ask me, a woman, for a

hot bed. Seem like you'd want to ask some nasty man like yourself for that."

"I thought about it, but I don't know no man live alone and it ain't nasty. Come on, girl. You driving me to the street. What I'm asking is better, ain't it? Every now and then I visit with a respectable lady."

"Respectable?"

"That's right, respectable. Maybe she's lonely though, or got children, or—"

"Or a husband with a hammer."

"Nobody like that."

"And if Violet finds out, what am I supposed to say?"

"She won't."

"Spose I tell her."

"You won't. Why would you do that? I'm still taking care of her. Nobody getting hurt. And you get two quarters as well as somebody looking out for your place while you gone in case Sweetness come back or somebody come in here looking for him and don't care what he tear up cause you a woman."

"Violet would kill me."

"You don't have nothing to do with it. You never know when I come and you won't see anything. Everything be like it was when you left, except if there's some little thing you want fixed you want me to do. You won't see nothing but some change on the table there that I leave for a reason you don't know nothing about, see?"

"Uh huh."

"Try me, Malvonne. One week. No, two. If you change your mind anytime, anytime, just leave my money on the table and I'll know you mean me to stop and sure as you live your door key will be laying in its place."

"Uh huh."

"It's your house. You tell me what you want done, what you want fixed, and you tell me what you don't like. But believe me, girl, you won't know when or if I come or go. Except, maybe, your faucet don't drip no more."

"Uh huh."

"Only thing you know is every Saturday, starting now, you got two more quarters to put in your sugar bowl."

"Mighty high price for a little conversation."

"You be surprised what you can save if you like me and don't drink, smoke, gamble or tithe."

"Maybe you should."

"I don't want nothing ornery, and I don't want to be hanging out in clubs and such. I just want some nice female company."

"You seem mighty sure you going to find it."

Joe smiled. "If I don't, still no harm. No harm at all."

"No messages."

"What?"

"No notes to pass. No letters. I'm not delivering any messages."

"Course not. I don't want a pen pal. We talk here or we don't talk at all."

"Suppose something comes up and you want or she wants to call it off?"

"Don't worry about that."

"Suppose she gets sick and can't come and needs to let you know."

"I wait, then I leave."

"Suppose one of the kids gets sick and can't nobody find the mama cause she holed up somewhere with you?"

"Who say she got kids?"

"Don't you take up with no woman if her kids is little, Joe."

"All right."

"It's asking too much of me."

"You don't have to think about none of it. You ain't in it. You ever see me mess with anybody? I been in this building longer than you have. You ever hear a word against me from any woman? I sell beauty products all over town, you ever hear tell of me chasing a woman? No. You never heard that, because it never happened. Now I'm trying to lighten my life a little with a good lady, like a decent man would, that's all. Tell me what's wrong with that?"

"Violet's wrong with it."

"Violet takes better care of her parrot than she does me. Rest of the time, she's cooking pork I can't eat, or pressing hair I can't stand the smell of. Maybe that's the way it goes with people been married long as we have. But the quiet. I can't take the quiet. She don't hardly talk anymore, and I ain't allowed near her. Any other man be running around, stepping out every night, you know that. I ain't like that. I ain't."

Of course he wasn't, but he did it anyway. Sneaked around, plotted, and stepped out every night the girl demanded. They went to Mexico, Sook's and clubs whose names changed every week—and he was not alone. He became a Thursday man and Thursday men are satisfied. I can tell from their look some outlaw love is about to be, or already has been, satisfied. Weekends and other days of the week are possibilities but Thursday is a day to be counted on. I used to think it was because domestic workers had Thursday off and could lie abed mornings as was out of the question on weekends, when either they slept in the houses they worked in or rose so early to arrive they had no time for breakfast or any kind of play. But I noticed it was also true of men whose women were not servants and day workers, but barmaids and restaurant cooks with Sunday-Monday free; schoolteachers, café singers, office typists and market-stall women all looked forward to Saturday off. The City thinks about and arranges itself for the weekend: the day before payday, the day after payday, the pre-Sabbath activity, the closed shop and the quiet school hall; barred bank vaults and offices locked in darkness.

So why is it on Thursday that the men look satisfied? Perhaps it's the artificial rhythm of the week—perhaps there is something so phony about the seven-day cycle the body pays no attention to it, preferring triplets, duets, quartets, anything but a cycle of seven that has to be broken into human parts and the break comes on Thursday. Irresistible. The outrageous expectations and inflexible demands of the weekend are null on Thursday. People look forward to weekends for connections, revisions and separations even though many of these activities are accompanied by bruises and even a spot of blood, for excitement runs high on Friday or Saturday.

But for satisfaction pure and deep, for balance in pleasure and comfort, Thursday can't be beat—as is clear from the capable expression on the faces of the men and their conquering stride in the street. They seem to achieve some sort of completion on that day that makes them steady enough on their feet to appear graceful even if they are not. They command the center of the sidewalk; whistle softly in unlit doors.

It doesn't last of course, and twenty-four hours later they are frightened again and restoring themselves with any helplessness within reach. So the weekends, destined to disappoint, are strident, sullen, sprinkled with bruises and dots of blood. The regrettable things, the coarse and sour remarks, the words that become active boils in the heart—none of that takes place on Thursday. I suppose the man for whom it is named would hate it, but the fact is, his day is a day for love in the City and the company of satisfied men. They make the women smile. The tunes whistled through perfect teeth are remembered, picked up later and repeated at the kitchen stove. In front of the mirror near the door one of them will turn her head to the side, and sway, enchanted with her waistline and the shape of her hips.

Up there, in that part of the City—which is the part they came for—the right tune whistled in a doorway or lifting up from the circles and grooves of a record can change the weather. From freezing to hot to cool.

Like that day in July, almost nine years back, when the beautiful men were cold. In typical summer weather, sticky and bright, Alice Manfred stood for three hours on Fifth Avenue marveling at the cold black faces and listening to drums saying what the graceful women and the marching men could not. What was possible to say was already in print on a banner that repeated a couple of promises from the Declaration of Independence and waved over the head of its bearer. But what was meant came from the drums. It was July in 1917 and the beautiful faces were cold and quiet; moving slowly into the space the drums were building for them.

During the march it seemed to Alice as though the day passed, the night too, and still she stood there, the hand of the little girl in her own, staring into each cold face that passed. The drums and the freezing faces hurt her, but hurt was better than fear and Alice had been frightened for a long time—first she was frightened of Illinois, then of Springfield, Massachusetts, then Eleventh Avenue, Third Avenue, Park Avenue. Recently she had begun to feel safe nowhere south of 110th Street, and Fifth Avenue was for her the most fearful of all. That was where whitemen leaned out of motor cars with folded dollar bills peeping from their palms. It was where salesmen touched her and only her as though she were part of the goods they had condescended to sell her; it was the tissue required if the management was generous enough to let you try on a blouse (but no hat) in a store. It was where she, a woman of fifty and independent means, had no surname. Where women who spoke English said, "Don't sit there, honey, you never know what they have." And women who knew no English at all and would never own a pair of silk stockings moved away from her if she sat next to them on the trolley.

Now, down Fifth Avenue from curb to curb, came a tide of cold black faces, speechless and unblinking because what they meant to say but did not trust themselves to say the drums said for them, and what they had seen with their own eyes and through the eyes of others the drums described to a T. The hurt hurt her, but the fear was gone at last. Fifth Avenue was put into focus now and so was her protection of the newly orphaned girl in her charge.

From then on she hid the girl's hair in braids tucked under, lest whitemen see it raining round her shoulders and push dollar-wrapped fingers toward her. She instructed her about deafness and blindness—how valuable and necessary they were in the company of whitewomen who spoke English and those who did not, as well as in the presence of their children. Taught her how to crawl along the walls of buildings, disappear into doorways, cut across corners in choked traffic—how to do anything, move anywhere to avoid a whiteboy over the age of eleven. Much of this she could effect with her dress, but as the girl grew older, more elaborate specifications had to be put in place. High-heeled shoes with the graceful straps across the arch, the vampy hats closed on the head with saucy brims framing the face, makeup of any kind—all of that was outlawed in Alice Manfred's house. Especially the coats slung low in the back and not buttoned, but clutched, like a bathrobe or a towel around the body, forcing the women who wore them to look like they had just stepped out of the bathtub and were already ready for bed.

Privately, Alice admired them, the coats and the women who wore them. She sewed linings into these coats, when she felt like working, and she had to look twice over her shoulder when the Gay Northeasters and the City Belles strolled down Seventh Avenue, they were so handsome. But this envy-streaked pleasure Alice closeted, and never let the girl see how she admired those ready-for-bed-in-the-street clothes. And she told the Miller sisters, who kept small children during the day for mothers who worked out of the house, what her feelings were. They did not need persuading, having been looking forward to the Day of Judgment for a dozen years, and expecting its sweet relief any minute now. They had lists of every restaurant, diner and club that sold liquor and were not above reporting owners and customers to the police until they discovered that such news, in the Racket Squad, was not only annoying, it was redundant.

When Alice Manfred collected the little girl from the Miller sisters, on those evenings following the days her fine stitching was solicited, the three women sat down in the kitchen to hum and sigh over cups of Postum at the signs of Imminent Demise: such as not just ankles but knees in full view; lip rouge red as hellfire; burnt matchsticks rubbed on eyebrows; fingernails tipped with blood—you couldn't tell the streetwalkers from the mothers. And the men, you know, the things they thought nothing of saying out loud to any woman who passed by could not be repeated before children. They did not know for sure, but they suspected that the dances were beyond nasty because the music was getting worse and worse with each passing season the Lord waited to make Himself known. Songs that used to start in the head and fill the heart had dropped on down, down to places below the sash and the buckled belts. Lower and lower, until the music was so lowdown you had to shut your windows and just suffer the summer sweat when the men in shirtsleeves propped themselves in window frames, or clustered on rooftops, in alleyways, on stoops and in the apartments of relatives playing the lowdown stuff that signaled Imminent Demise. Or when a woman with a baby on her shoulder and a skillet in her hand sang "Turn to my pillow where my sweetman used to be . . . how long, how long, how long." Because you could hear it everywhere. Even if you lived, as Alice Manfred and the Miller sisters did, on Clifton Place, with a leafy sixty-foot tree every hundred feet, a quiet street with no fewer than five motor cars parked at the curb, you could still hear it, and there was no mistaking what it did to the children under their care—cocking their heads and swaying ridiculous, unformed hips.

Alice thought the lowdown music (and in Illinois it was worse than here) had something to do with the silent black women and men marching down Fifth Avenue to advertise their anger over two hundred dead in East St. Louis, two of whom were her sister and brother-in-law, killed in the riots. So many whites killed the papers would not print the number.

Some said the rioters were disgruntled veterans who had fought in all-colored units, were refused the services of the YMCA, over there and over here, and came home to white violence more intense than when they enlisted and, unlike the battles they fought in Europe, stateside fighting was pitiless and totally without honor. Others said they were whites terrified by the wave of southern Negroes flooding the towns, searching for work and places to live. A few thought about it and said how perfect was the control of workers, none of whom (like crabs in a barrel requiring no lid, no stick, not even a monitoring observation) would get out of the barrel.

Alice, however, believed she knew the truth better than everybody. Her brother-in-law was not a veteran, and he had been living in East St. Louis since before the War. Nor did he need a whiteman's job—he owned a pool hall. As a matter of fact, he wasn't even in the riot; he had no weapons, confronted nobody on the street. He was pulled off a streetcar and stomped to death, and Alice's sister had just got the news and had gone back home to try and forget the color of his entrails, when her house was torched and she burned crispy in its flame. Her only child, a little girl named Dorcas, sleeping across the road with her very best girlfriend, did not hear the fire engine clanging and roaring down the street because when it was called it didn't come. But she must have seen the flames, must have, because the whole street was screaming. She never said. Never said anything about it. She went to two funerals in five days, and never said a word.

Alice thought, No. It wasn't the War and the disgruntled veterans; it wasn't the droves and droves of colored people flocking to paychecks and streets full of themselves. It was the music. The dirty, get-on-down music the women sang and the men played and both danced to, close and shameless or apart and wild. Alice was convinced and so were the Miller sisters as they blew into cups of Postum in the kitchen. It made you do unwise disorderly things. Just hearing it was like violating the law.

There had been none of that at the Fifth Avenue march. Just the drums and the Colored Boy Scouts passing out explanatory leaflets to whitemen in straw hats who needed to know what the freezing faces already knew. Alice had picked up a leaflet that had floated to the pavement, read the words, and shifted her weight at the curb. She read the words and looked at Dorcas. Looked at Dorcas and read the words again. What she read seemed crazy, out of focus. Some great gap lunged between the print and the child. She glanced between them struggling for the connection, something to close the distance between the silent staring child and the slippery crazy words. Then suddenly, like a rope cast for rescue, the drums spanned the distance, gathering them all up and connected them: Alice, Dorcas, her sister and her brother-in-law, the Boy Scouts and the frozen black faces, the watchers on the pavement and those in the windows above.

Alice carried that gathering rope with her always after that day on Fifth Avenue, and found it reliably secure and tight—most of the time. Except when the men sat on windowsills fingering horns, and the women wondered "how long." The rope broke then, disturbing her peace, making her aware of flesh and something so free she could smell its bloodsmell; made her aware of its life below the sash and its red lip rouge.

She knew from sermons and editorials that it wasn't real music—just colored folks' stuff: harmful, certainly; embarrassing, of course; but not real, not serious.

Yet Alice Manfred swore she heard a complicated anger in it; something hostile that disguised itself as flourish and roaring seduction. But the part she hated most was its appetite. Its longing for the bash, the slit; a kind of careless hunger for a fight or a red ruby stickpin for a tie—either would do. It faked happiness, faked welcome, but it did not make her feel generous, this juke joint, barrel hooch, tonk house, music. It made her hold her hand in the pocket of her apron to keep from smashing it through the glass pane to snatch the world in her fist and squeeze the life out of it for doing what it did and did and did to her and everybody else she knew or knew about. Better to close the windows and the shutters, sweat in the summer heat of a silent Clifton Place apartment than to risk a broken window or a yelping that might not know where or how to stop.

I have seen her, passing a café or an uncurtained window when some phrase or other—"Hit me but don't quit me"—drifted out, and watched her reach with one hand for the safe gathering rope thrown to her eight years ago on Fifth Avenue, and ball the other one into a fist in her coat pocket. I don't know how she did it—balance herself with two different hand gestures. But she was not alone in trying, and she was not alone in losing. It was impossible to keep the Fifth Avenue drums separate from the belt-buckle tunes vibrating from pianos and spinning on every Victrola. Impossible. Some nights are silent; not a motor car turning within earshot; no drunks or restless babies crying for their mothers and Alice opens any window she wants to and hears nothing at all.

Wondering at this totally silent night, she can go back to bed but as soon as she turns the pillow to its smoother, cooler side, a melody line she doesn't remember where from sings itself, loud and unsolicited, in her head. "When I was young and in my prime I could get my barbecue any old time." They are greedy, reckless words, loose and infuriating, but hard to dismiss because underneath, holding up the looseness like a palm, are the drums that put Fifth Avenue into focus.

Her niece, of course, didn't have the problem. Alice had been reraising her, correcting her, since the summer of 1917, and although her earliest memory when she arrived from East St. Louis was the parade her aunt took her to, a kind of funeral parade for her mother and her father, Dorcas remembered it differently. While her aunt worried about how to keep the heart ignorant of the hips and the head in charge of both, Dorcas lay on a chenille bedspread, tickled and happy knowing that there was no place to be where somewhere, close by, somebody was not licking his licorice stick, tickling the ivories, beating his skins, blowing off his horn while a knowing woman sang ain't nobody going to keep me down you got the right key baby but the wrong keyhole you got to get it bring it and put it right here, or else.

Resisting her aunt's protection and restraining hands, Dorcas thought of that life-below-the-sash as all the life there was. The drums she heard at the parade were only the first part, the first word, of a command. For her the drums were not an all-embracing rope of fellowship, discipline and transcendence. She remembered them as a beginning, a start of something she looked to complete.

Back in East St. Louis, as the little porch fell, wood chips—ignited and smoking—exploded in the air. One of them must have entered her stretched dumb mouth and traveled down her throat because it smoked and glowed there still. Dorcas never let it out and never put it out. At first she thought if she spoke of it, it would leave her, or she would lose it through her mouth. And when her aunt took her on a train to the City, and crushed her hand while they watched a long parade, the bright wood chip sank further and further down until it lodged comfortably somewhere below her navel. She watched the black unblinking men, and the drums assured her that the glow would never leave her, that it would be waiting for and with her whenever she wanted to be touched by it. And whenever she wanted to let it loose to leap into fire again, whatever happened would be quick. Like the dolls.

They would have gone fast. Wood, after all, in a wooden cigar box. The red tissue-paper skirt on Rochelle immediately. Sst, like a match, and then Bernadine's blue silk and Faye's white cotton cape. The fire would eat away at their legs, blacken them first with its hot breath and their round eyes, with the tiny lashes and eyebrows she had painted in so very carefully, would have watched themselves disappear. Dorcas avoided thinking about the huge coffin just there in front, a few feet to her left, and about the medicinal odor of Aunt Alice sitting next to her, by concentrating on Rochelle and Bernadine and Faye, who would have no funeral at all. It made her bold. Even as a nine-year-old in elementary school she was bold. However tight and tucked in her braids, however clunky her high-topped shoes that covered ankles other girls exposed in low-cut oxfords, however black and thick her stockings, nothing hid the boldness swaying under her cast-iron skirt. Eyeglasses could not obscure it, nor could the pimples on her skin brought on by hard brown soap and a tilted diet.

When she was little, and Alice Manfred agreed to sew for

a month or two, Dorcas was watched over after school by the Miller sisters. Often there were four other children, sometimes one other. Their play was quiet and confined to a small area of the dining room. The two-armed sister, Frances Miller, gave them apple-butter sandwiches to eat; the one-armed one, Neola, read them Psalms. The strict discipline was occasionally lightened when Frances napped at the kitchen table. Then Neola might grow tired of the constraint the verses imposed on her own voice and select a child to light a match for her cigarette. She would take fewer than three puffs, and something in the gesture stirred something inside her, and she told her charges cautionary tales. Her stories, however, of the goodness of good behavior collapsed before the thrill of the sin they deplored.

The truth is that the message in her instructions failed because a week after he put the engagement ring on Neola's finger, the soon-to-be-groom at her wedding left the state. The pain of his refusal was visual, for over her heart, curled like a shell, was the hand on which he had positioned the ring. As though she held the broken pieces of her heart together in the crook of a frozen arm. No other part of her was touched by this paralysis. Her right hand, the one that turned the tissue-thin pages of the Old Testament, or held an Old Gold cigarette to her lips, was straight and steady. But the stories she told them of moral decay, of the wicked who preyed on the good, were made more poignant by this clutch of arm to breast. She told them how she had personally advised a friend to respect herself and leave the man who was no good to (or for) her. Finally the friend agreed but in two days, two! she went right back to him God help us all, and Neola never spoke to her again. She told them how a very young girl, no more than fourteen, had left family and friends to traipse four hundred miles after a boy who joined the army only to be left behind and turn to a completely dissolute life in a camptown. So they could see, couldn't they, the power of sin in the company of a weak mind? The children scratched their knees and nodded, but Dorcas, at least, was enchanted by the frail, melty tendency of the flesh and the Paradise that could make a woman go right back after two days, two! or make a girl travel four hundred miles to a camptown, or fold Neola's arm, the better to hold the pieces of her heart in her hand. Paradise. All for Paradise.

By the time she was seventeen her whole life was unbearable. And when I think about it, I know just how she felt. It is terrible when there is absolutely nothing to do or worth doing except to lie down and hope when you are naked she won't laugh at you. Or that he, holding your breasts, won't wish they were some other way. Terrible but worth the risk, because there is no other thing to do, although, being seventeen, you do it. Study, work, memorize. Bite into food and the reputations of your friends. Laugh at the things that are right side up and those that are upside-down—it doesn't matter because you are not doing the thing worth doing which is lying down somewhere in a dimly lit place enclosed in arms, and supported by the core of the world.

Think how it is, if you can manage, just manage it. Nature freaks for you, then. Turns itself into shelter, byways. Pillows for two. Spreads the limbs of lilac bushes low enough to hide you. And the City, in its own way, gets down for you, cooperates, smoothing its sidewalks, correcting its curbstones, offering you melons and green apples on the corner. Racks of yellow head scarves; strings of Egyptian beads. Kansas fried chicken and something with raisins call attention to an open window where the aroma seems to lurk. And if that's not enough, doors to speakeasies stand ajar and in that cool dark place a clarinet coughs and clears its throat waiting for the woman to decide on the key. She makes up her mind and as you pass by informs your back that she is daddy's little angel child. The City is smart at this: smelling and good and looking raunchy; sending secret messages disguised as public signs: this way, open here, danger to let colored only single men on sale woman wanted private room stop dog on premises absolutely no money down fresh chicken free delivery fast. And good at opening locks, dimming stairways. Covering your moans with its own.

There was a night in her sixteenth year when Dorcas stood in her body and offered it to either of the brothers for a dance. Both boys were shorter than she, but both were equally attractive. More to the point, they outstepped everybody so completely that when they needed tough competition they were forced to dance with themselves. Sneaking out to that party with her best friend, Felice, ought to have been hard to arrange, but Alice Manfred had overnight business in Springfield, and nothing could have been easier. The only difficulty was in finding something foxy enough to wear.

The two girlfriends climb the stairs, led straight to the right place more by the stride piano pouring over the door saddle than their recollection of the apartment number. They pause to exchange looks before knocking. Even in the dim hallway the dark-skinned friend heightens the cream color of the other. Felice's oily hair enhances Dorcas' soft, dry waves. The door opens and they step in.

Before the lights are turned out, and before the sandwiches and the spiked soda water disappear, the one managing the record player chooses fast music suitable for the brightly lit room, where obstructing furniture has been shoved against walls, pushed into the hallway, and bedrooms piled high with coats. Under the ceiling light pairs move like twins born with, if not for, the other, sharing a partner's pulse like a second jugular. They believe they know before the music does what their hands, their feet are to do, but that illusion is the music's secret drive: the control it tricks them into believing is theirs; the anticipation it anticipates. In between record changes, while the girls fan blouse necks to air damp collarbones or pat with anxious hands the damage moisture has done to their hair, the boys press folded handkerchiefs to their foreheads. Laughter covers indiscreet glances of welcome and promise, and takes the edge off gestures of betrayal and abandon.

Dorcas and Felice are not strangers at the party—nobody is. People neither of them has seen before join the fun as easily as those who have grown up in the building. But both girls have expectations made higher by the trouble they'd had planning outfits for the escapade. Dorcas, at sixteen, has yet to wear silk hose and her shoes are those of someone much younger or very old. Felice has helped her loosen two braids behind her ears and her fingertip is stained with the rouge she has stroked across her lips. With her collar turned under, her dress is more adult-looking, but the hard hand of a warning grown-up shows everywhere else: in the hem, the waist-centered belt, the short, puffy sleeves. She and Felice have tried removing the belt altogether, then fixing it at her navel. Both strategies prove hateful. They know that a badly dressed body is nobody at all, and Felice had to chatter compliments all the way down Seventh Avenue to get Dorcas to forget about her clothes and focus on the party.

Music soars to the ceiling and through the windows wide

open for circulation as they enter. Immediately both girls are snatched by male hands and spun into the dancing center of the room. Dorcas recognizes her partner as Martin, who had been in her elocution class for a hot minute—which was as long as it took for the teacher to realize he would never relinquish "ax" for "ask." Dorcas dances well—not as fast as some others, but she is graceful, in spite of those shaming shoes, and she is provocative.

It is after two more dances that she notices the brothers commanding the attention of a crowd in the dining room. On the street, in vestibules as well as house parties, they are spectacular, moving like taut silk or loose metal. The stomach-jump Dorcas and Felice have agreed is the Sign of real interest and possible love surfaces and spreads as Dorcas watches the brothers. The sandwiches are gone now, the potato salad too, and everybody knows that the time for lights-out music is approaching. The unbelievable agility, the split-second timing the brothers are putting on display announces the culmination of the fast-dancing segment of the party.

Dorcas moves into the hall that parallels the living and dining room. From its shadows, through the archway, she has an unrestricted view of the brothers as they bring the performance to its rousing close. Laughing, they accept the praise that is due them: adoring looks from girls, congratulating punches and slaps from the boys. They have wonderful faces, these brothers. Their smiles, more than flawless teeth, are amused and inviting. Someone fights with the Victrola; places the arm on, scratches the record, tries again, then exchanges the record for another. During the lull, the brothers notice Dorcas. Taller than most, she gazes at them over the head of her dark friend. The brothers' eyes seem wide and welcoming to her. She moves forward out of the shadow and slips through the group. The brothers turn up the wattage of their smiles. The right record is on the turntable now; she can hear its preparatory hiss as the needle slides toward its first groove. The brothers smile brilliantly; one leans a fraction of an inch toward the other and, never losing eye contact with Dorcas, whispers something. The other looks Dorcas up and down as she moves toward them. Then, just as the music, slow and smoky, loads up the air, his smile bright as ever, he wrinkles his nose and turns away.

Dorcas has been acknowledged, appraised and dismissed in the time it takes for a needle to find its opening groove. The stomach-jump of possible love is nothing compared to the ice floes that block up her veins now. The body she inhabits is unworthy. Although it is young and all she has, it is as if it had decayed on the vine at budding time. No wonder Neola closed her arm and held the pieces of her heart in her hand.

So by the time Joe Trace whispered to her through the crack of a closing door her life had become almost unbearable. Almost. The flesh, heavily despised by the brothers, held secret the love appetite soaring inside it. I've seen swollen fish, serenely blind, floating in the sky. Without eyes, but somehow directed, these airships swim below cloud foam and nobody can be turned away from the sight of them because it's like watching a private dream. That was what her hunger was like: mesmerizing, directed, floating like a public secret just under the cloud cover. Alice Manfred had worked hard to privatize her niece, but she was no match for a City seeping music that begged and challenged each and every day. "Come," it said. "Come and do wrong." Even the grandmothers sweeping the stairs closed their eyes and held their heads back as they celebrated their sweet desolation. "Nobody does me like you do me." In the year that passed between the dancing brothers' dismissal and Alice Manfred's club meeting, the yoke Alice had knotted around Dorcas' neck frayed till it split.

Other than the clubwomen, very few knew where Joe Trace met her. Not at the candy counter of Duggie's where he first saw her and wondered if that, the peppermint she bought, was what insulted her skin, light and creamy everywhere but her cheeks. Joe met Dorcas in Alice Manfred's house right up under her nose and right before her very eyes.

He had gone there to deliver an order to Malvonne Edwards' cousin Sheila who said if Joe came to 237 Clifton Place before noon he could deliver her order, the #2 Nut Brown and the vanishing cream, right there, and she wouldn't have to wait till the following Saturday or walk all the way over to Lenox at night to pick it up, unless, of course, he wanted to come on her job. . . .

Joe had decided he would wait till next Saturday because not collecting the dollar and thirty-five cents wasn't going to strap him. But after he left Miss Ransom's house and stood for a half hour watching Bud and C.T. abusing each other at checkers, he decided to check Sheila out right fast and quit for the day. His stomach was a bit sour and his feet already hurt. He didn't want to be caught delivering or writing orders in the rain either, rain that had been threatening all during that warm October morning. And even though getting home early meant the extended company of a speechless Violet while he fussed with the sink trap or the pulley that turned the clothesline on their side of the building, the Saturday meal would be early too and satisfying: late summer greens cooked with the ham bone left over from last Sunday. Joe looked forward to the lean, scrappy end-of-week meals, but hated the Sunday one: a baked ham, a sweet heavy pie to follow it. Violet's determination to grow an ass she swore she once owned was killing him.

Once upon a time, he bragged about her cooking. Couldn't wait to get back to the house and devour it. But he was fifty now, and appetites change, we know. He still liked candy, hard candy—not divinity or caramel—sour balls being his favorite. If Violet would confine herself to soup and boiled vegetables (with a bit of bread to go along) he would be perfectly satisfied.

That's what he was thinking about when he found 237 and climbed the stairs. The argument between C.T. and Bud over the fate of S.S. *Ethiopia* had been too good, too funny: he had listened to them longer than he thought, because it was way past noon when he got there. Woman noise could be heard through the door. Joe rang anyway.

The peppermint girl with the bad skin answered the door, and while he was telling her who he was and what he'd come for, Sheila poked her head into the vestibule and shouted, "CPT! Surprise me for once, Joe Trace." He smiled and stepped in the door. Stood there smiling and did not put his sample case down until the hostess, Alice Manfred, came and told him to come on in the parlor.

They were thrilled to have him interrupt their social. It was a luncheon meeting of the Civic Daughters to plan for the Thanksgiving fund raiser for the National Negro Business League. They had settled what they could, tabled what they had to, and begun the chicken à la king lunch over which Alice had taken the greatest pains. Pleased, happy even, with their work and with each other's company, they did not know they were missing anything until Alice sent Dorcas to answer the ring, and Sheila, remembering what she had said to Joe, jumped up when she heard a male voice.

They made him feel like the singing men in spats. The

young ones who clustered on the corners wearing ties the color of handkerchiefs sticking out of their breast pockets. The young roosters who stood without waiting for the chicks who were waiting—for them. Under the women's flirty, appraising eyes, Joe felt the pleasure of his own smile as though sand-colored spats covered his shoe tops.

They laughed, tapped the tablecloth with their fingertips and began to tease, berate and adore him all at once. They told him how tall men like him made them feel, complained about his lateness and insolence, asked him what *else* he had in his case besides whatever it was that made Sheila so excited. They wondered why he never rang *their* doorbells, or climbed four flights of double-flight stairs to deliver anything to them. They sang their compliments, their abuse, and only Alice confined herself to a thin smile, a closed look, and did not join the comments with one of her own.

Of course he stayed to lunch. Of course. Although he tried not to eat anything much and spoil his appetite for the late-summer greens he was sure were simmering in the pot for him. But the women touched his hair and looked right at him, musing over his two-color eyes and ordered him: "Come on over here, man, and sit yourself down. Fix you a plate? Let me fix you a plate." He protested; they insisted. He opened his case; they offered to buy him out. "Eat, baby, eat," they said. "You not going out in that pneumonia weather without something sticking to your bones don't make no sense with all we got here, Dorcas, girl, bring this man a empty plate so I can fill it for him hear? Hush, Sheila."

They were women his age mostly, with husbands, children, grandchildren too. Hard workers for themselves and anyone who needed them. And they thought men were ridiculous and delicious and terrible, taking every opportunity to let them know that they were. In a group such as this one, they could do with impunity what they were cautious about alone with any man, stranger or friend, who rang the doorbell with a sample case in his hand, no matter how tall he was, how country his smile or however much sadness was in his eyes. Besides, they liked his voice. It had a pitch, a note they heard only when they visited stubborn old folks who would not budge from their front yards and overworked fields to come to the City. It reminded them of men who wore hats to plow and to eat supper in; who blew into saucers of coffee, and held knives in their fists when they ate. So they looked right at him and told him any way they could how ridiculous he was, and how delicious and how terrible. As if he didn't know.

Joe Trace counted on flirty laughing women to buy his wares, and he knew better than to take up with any of them. Not if he wanted to be able to lean over a pool table for a shot exposing his back to his customers' husbands. But that day in Alice Manfred's house, as he listened to and returned their banter, something in the wordplay took on weight.

I've wondered about it. What he thought then and later, and about what he said to her. He whispered something to Dorcas when she let him out the door, and nobody looked more pleased and surprised than he did.

If I remember right, that October lunch in Alice Manfred's house, something was off. Alice was vague and anybody in her company for thirty minutes knew that wasn't her style. She was the one who with a look could cut good gossip down to a titter when it got out of hand. And maybe it was her head-of-a-seamstress head that made what you thought was a cheerful dress turn loud and tatty next to hers. But she could lay a table.

Food might be a tad skimpy in the portions, and I believe she had a prejudice against butter, she used so little of it in her cakes. But the biscuits were light, and the plates, the flatware, sparkling and arranged just so. Open her napkins wide as you please and not a catface anywhere. She was polite at the lunch of course; not too haughty either, but not paying close attention to things. Distracted she was. About Dorcas, probably.

I always believed that girl was a pack of lies. I could tell by her walk her underclothes were beyond her years, even if her dress wasn't. Maybe back in October Alice was beginning to think so too. By the time January came, nobody had to speculate. Everybody knew. I wonder if she had a premonition of Joe Trace knocking on her door? Or it could have been something she read in all those newspapers stacked neatly along the baseboard in her bedroom.

Everybody needs a pile of newspapers: to peel potatoes on, serve bathroom needs, wrap garbage. But not like Alice Manfred. She must have read them over and over else why would she keep them? And if she read anything in the newspaper twice she knew too little about too much. If you have secrets you want kept or want to figure out those other people have, a newspaper can turn your mind. The best thing to find out what's going on is to watch how people maneuver themselves in the streets. What sidewalk preachers stop them in their tracks? Do they walk right through the boys kicking cans along the sidewalk or holler at them to quit? Ignore the men sitting on car fenders or stop to exchange a word? If a fight breaks out between a man and a woman do they cross in the middle of the block to watch or run to the corner in case it gets messy?

One thing for sure, the streets will confuse you, teach you or break your head. But Alice Manfred wasn't the kind to give herself reasons to be in the streets. She got through them quick as she could to get back to her house. If she had come out more often, sat on the stoop or gossiped in front of the beauty shop, she would have known more than what the paper said. She might have known what was happening under her nose. When she did find out what took place between that October day and the awful January one that ended everything, the last people on earth she wanted to see was Joe Trace or anybody connected to him. It happened, though. The woman who avoided the streets let into her living room the woman who sat down in the middle of one.

Toward the end of March, Alice Manfred put her needles aside to think again of what she called the *impunity* of the man who killed her niece just because he could. It had not been hard to do; it had not even made him think twice about what danger he was putting himself in. He just did it. One man. One defenseless girl. Death. A sample-case man. A nice, neighborly, everybody-knows-him man. The kind you let in your house because he was not dangerous, because you had seen him with children, bought his products and never heard a scrap of gossip about him doing wrong. Felt not only safe but kindly in his company because he was the sort women ran to when they thought they were being followed, or watched or needed someone to have the extra key just in case you locked yourself out. He was the man who took you to your door if you missed the trolley and had to walk night streets at night. Who warned young girls away from hooch joints and the men who lingered there. Women teased him because they trusted him. He was one of those men who might have marched down Fifth Avenue—cold and silent and dignified—into the space the drums made. He *knew* wrong wasn't right, and did it anyway.

Alice Manfred had seen and borne much, had been scared all over the country, in every street of it. Only now did she feel truly unsafe because the brutalizing men and their brutal women were not just out there, they were in her block, her house. A man had come in her living room and destroyed her niece. His wife had come right in the funeral to nasty and dishonor her. She would have called the police after both of them if everything she knew about Negro life had made it even possible to consider. To actually volunteer to talk to one, black or white, to let him in her house, watch him adjust his hips in her chair to accommodate the blue steel that made him a man.

Idle and withdrawn in her grief and shame, she whittled away the days making lace for nothing, reading her newspapers, tossing them on the floor, picking them up again. She read them differently now. Every week since Dorcas' death, during the whole of January and February, a paper laid bare the bones of some broken woman. Man kills wife. Eight accused of rape dismissed. Woman and girl victims of. Woman commits suicide. White attackers indicted. Five women caught. Woman says man beat. In jealous rage man.

Defenseless as ducks, she thought. Or were they? Read carefully the news accounts revealed that most of these women, subdued and broken, had not been defenseless. Or, like Dorcas, easy prey. All over the country, black women were armed. That, thought Alice, that, at least, they had learned. Didn't everything on God's earth have or acquire defense? Speed, some poison in the leaf, the tongue, the tail? A mask, flight, numbers in the millions producing numbers in the millions? A thorn here, a spike there.

Natural prey? Easy pickings? "I don't think so." Aloud she said it. "I don't think so."

Worn spots in the linen had been strengthened with 60-weight thread. Laundered and folded it lay in a basket her mother had used. Alice raised the ironing board and spread newspaper under it to keep the hems clean. She was waiting not only for the irons to heat but also for a brutal woman black as soot known to carry a knife. She waited with less hesitation than she had before and with none of the scary angry feelings she had in January when a woman saying she was Violet Trace had tried to see her, talk or something. Knocked on her door so early in the morning Alice thought it was the law.

"I don't have a thing to say to you. Not one thing." She had said it in a loud whisper through the chained opening in the door and slammed it shut. She didn't need the name to be afraid or to know who she was: the star of her niece's funeral. The woman who ruined the service, changed the whole point and meaning of it and was practically all anybody talked about when they talked about Dorcas' death and in the process had changed the woman's name. Violent they called her now. No wonder. Alice, sitting in the first seat in the first aisle had watched the church commotion stunned. Later, and little by little, feelings, like sea trash expelled on a beach—strange and recognizable, stark and murky—returned.

Chief among them was fear and—a new thing—anger. At Joe Trace who had been the one who did it: seduced her niece right under her nose in her very own house. The nice one. The man who sold ladies' products on the side; a familiar figure in just about every building in town. A man store owners and landlords liked because he set the children's toys in a neat row when they left them scattered on the sidewalk. Who the children liked because he never minded them. And liked among men because he never cheated in a game, egged a stupid fight on, or carried tales, and he left their women alone. Liked among the women because he made them feel like girls; liked by girls because he made them feel like women—which, she thought, was what Dorcas was looking for. Murderer.

But Alice wasn't afraid of him nor, now, his wife. For Joe she felt trembling fury at his snake-in-the-grass stealing of the girl in her charge; and shame that the grass he had snaked through was her own—the watched and guarded environment where unmarried and unmarriageable pregnancy was the end and close of livable life. After that—zip. Just a wait until the baby that came was old enough to warrant its own watched, guarded environment.

Waiting for Violet, with less hesitation than before, Alice wondered why it was so. At fifty-eight with no children of her own, and the one she had access to and responsibility for dead, she wondered about the hysteria, the violence, the damnation of pregnancy without marriageability. It had occupied her own parents' mind completely for as long as she could remember them. They spoke to her firmly but carefully about her body: sitting nasty (legs open); sitting womanish (legs crossed); breathing through her mouth; hands on hips; slumping at table; switching when you walked. The moment she got breasts they were bound and resented, a resentment that increased to outright hatred of her pregnant possibilities and never stopped until she married Louis Manfred, when suddenly it was the opposite. Even before the wedding her parents were murmuring about grandchildren they could see and hold, while at the same time and in turn resenting the tips showing and growing under the chemises of Alice's younger sisters. Resenting the blood spots, the new hips, the hair. That and the necessity for new clothes. "Oh, Lord, girl!" The frown when the hem could not be taken down further; the waistband refused another stitch. Growing up under that heated control, Alice swore she wouldn't, but she did, pass it on. She passed it on to her baby sister's only child. And wondered now would she have done so had her husband lived or stayed or if she had had children of her own. If he had been there, by her side, helping her make decisions, maybe she would not be sitting there waiting for a woman called Violent and thinking war thoughts. Although war was what it was. Which is why she had chosen surrender and made Dorcas her own prisoner of war.

Other women, however, had not surrendered. All over the country they were armed. Alice worked once with a Swedish tailor who had a scar from his earlobe to the corner of his mouth. "Negress," he said. "She cut me to the teeth, to the teeth." He smiled his wonder and shook his head. "To the teeth." The iceman in Springfield had four evenly spaced holes in the side of his neck from four evenly spaced jabs by something thin, round and sharp. Men ran through the streets of Springfield, East St. Louis and the City holding one red wet hand in the other, a flap of skin on the face. Sometimes they got to a hospital safely alive only because they left the razor where it lodged.

Black women were armed; black women were dangerous and the less money they had the deadlier the weapon they chose.

Who were the unarmed ones? Those who found protection in church and the judging, angry God whose wrath in their behalf was too terrible to bear contemplation. He was not just on His way, coming, coming to right the wrongs done to them, He was here. Already. See? See? What the world had done to them it was now doing to itself. Did the world mess over them? Yes but look where the mess originated. Were they berated and cursed? Oh yes but look how the world cursed and berated itself. Were the women fondled in kitchens and the back of stores? Uh huh. Did police put their fists in women's faces so the husbands' spirits would break along with the women's jaws? Did men (those who knew them as well as strangers sitting in motor cars) call them out of their names every single day of their lives? Uh huh. But in God's eyes and theirs, every hateful word and gesture was the Beast's desire for its own filth. The Beast did not do what was done to it, but what it wished done to itself: raped because it wanted to be raped itself. Slaughtered children because it yearned to be slaughtered children. Built jails to dwell on and hold on to its own private decay. God's wrath, so beautiful, so simple. Their enemies got what they wanted, became what they visited on others.

Who else were the unarmed ones? The ones who thought they did not need folded blades, packets of lye, shards of glass taped to their hands. Those who bought houses and hoarded money as protection and the means to purchase it. Those attached to armed men. Those who did not carry pistols because they became pistols; did not carry switchblades because they were switchblades cutting through gatherings, shooting down statutes and pointing out the blood and abused flesh. Those who swelled their little unarmed strength into the reckoning one of leagues, clubs, societies, sisterhoods designed to hold or withhold, move or stay put, make a way, solicit, comfort and ease. Bail out, dress the dead, pay the rent, find new rooms, start a school, storm an office, take up collections, rout the block and keep their eyes on all the children. Any other kind of unarmed black woman in 1926 was silent or crazy or dead.

Alice waited this time, in the month of March, for the woman with the knife. The woman people called Violent now because she had tried to kill what lay in a coffin. She had left notes under Alice's door every day beginning in January—a week after the funeral—and Alice Manfred knew the kind of Negro that couple was: the kind she trained Dorcas away from. The embarrassing kind. More than unappealing, they were dangerous. The husband shot; the wife stabbed. Nothing. Nothing her niece did or tried could equal the violence done to her. And where there was violence wasn't there also vice? Gambling. Cursing. A terrible and nasty closeness. Red dresses. Yellow shoes. And, of course, race music to urge them on.

But Alice was not frightened of her now as she had been in January and as she was in February, the first time she let her in. She'd thought the woman would end up in jail one day—they all did eventually. But easy pickings? Natural prey? "I don't think so. I don't think so."

At the wake, Malvonne gave her the details. Tried to, anyway. Alice leaned away from the woman and held her breath as though to keep the words at bay.

"I appreciate your concern," Alice told her. "Help yourself." She gestured toward tables crowded with food and the well-wishers circling it. "There's so much."

"I feel so bad," Malvonne said. "Like it was my own."

"Thank you."

"You raise other people's children and it hurts just the same as it would if it was your own. You know about Sweetness, my nephew . . . ?"

"Excuse me."

"Did everything for him. Everything a mother would."

"Please. Help yourself. There's so much. Too much."

"Those old reprobates, they live in my building, you know. . . ."

"Hello, Felice. Nice of you to come . . ."

She did not want to hear or know too much then. And she did not want to see that woman they began to call Violent either. The note she slid under Alice's door offended her, then frightened her. But after a while, having heard how torn up the man was and reading the headlines in the *Age,* the *News, The Messenger,* by February she had steeled herself and let the woman in.

"What *could* you want from me?"

"Oh, right now I just want to sit down on your chair," Violet said.

"I'm sorry. I just can't think what good can come of this."

"I'm having trouble with my head," said Violet placing her fingers on the crown of her hat.

"See a doctor, why don't you?"

Violet walked past her, drawn like a magnet to a small side table. "Is that her?"

Alice didn't have to look to know what she was staring at.

"Yes."

The long pause that followed, while Violet examined the face that loomed out of the frame, made Alice nervous. Before she got up the courage to ask the woman to leave, she turned away from the photograph saying, "I'm not the one you need to be scared of."

"No? Who is?"

"I don't know. That's what hurts my head."

"You didn't come here to say you sorry. I thought maybe you did. You come in here to deliver some of your own evil."

"I don't have no evil of my own."

"I think you'd better go."

"Let me rest here a minute. I can't find a place where I can just sit down. That's her there?"

"I just told you it was."

"She give you a lot of trouble?"

"No. None. Well. Some."

"I was a good girl her age. Never gave a speck of trouble. I did everything anybody told me to. Till I got here. City make you tighten up."

Odd-acting, thought Alice, but not bloody-minded. And before she could think not to let it happen, the question was out. "Why did he do such a thing?"

"Why did she?"

"Why did you?"

"I don't know."

The second time she came, Alice was still pondering over those wild women with their packets of lye, their honed razors, the keloids here, here and there. She was pulling the curtain to cut off the light that smashed right into her visitor's eyes when she said, "Your husband. Does he hurt you?"

"Hurt me?" Violet looked puzzled.

"I mean he seemed so nice, so quiet. Did he beat on you?"

"Joe? No. He never hurt nothing."

"Except Dorcas."

"And squirrels."

"What?"

"Rabbits too. Deer. Possum. Pheasant. We ate good down home."

"Why'd you leave?"

"Landowner didn't want rabbit. He want soft money."

"They want money here, too."

"But there's a way to get it here. I did day work when I first came here. Three houses a day got me good money. Joe cleaned fish at night. Took a while before he got hotel work. I got into hairdressing, and Joe . . ."

"I don't want to hear about all that."

Violet shut up and stared at the photograph. Alice gave it to her to get her out of the house.

The next day she was back and looked so bad Alice wanted to slap her. Instead she said, "Take that dress off and I'll stitch up your cuff." Violet wore the same dress each time and Alice was irritated by the thread running loose from her sleeve, as well as the coat lining ripped in at least three places she could see.

Violet sat in her slip with her coat on, while Alice mended the sleeve with the tiniest stitches. At no time did Violet take off her hat.

"At first I thought you came here to harm me. Then I thought you wanted to offer condolences. Then I thought you wanted to thank me for not calling the law. But none of that is it, is it?"

"I had to sit down somewhere. I thought I could do it here. That you would let me and you did. I know I didn't give Joe much reason to stay out of the street. But I wanted to see what kind of girl he'd rather me be."

"Foolish. He'd rather you were eighteen, that's all."

"No. Something more."

"You don't know anything about your own husband, I can't be expected to help you."

"You didn't know they were seeing each other no more than I did and you saw her every day like I did Joe. I know where my mind was. Where was yours?"

"Don't chastise me. I won't let you do that."

. . .

Alice had finished the sheets and begun the first shirtwaist when Violet knocked on her door. Years and years and years ago she had guided the tip of the iron into the seams of a man's white shirt. Dampened just so the fabric smoothed and tightened with starch. Those shirts were scraps now. Dust cloths, monthly cloths, rags tied around pipe joints to hinder freezing; pot holders and pieces to test hot irons and wrap their handles. Even wicks for oil lamps; salt bags to scrub the teeth. Now her own shirtwaists got her elegant attentive handcare.

Two pairs of pillow slips, still warm to the touch, were stacked on the table. So were the two bed sheets. Next week, perhaps, the curtains.

By now she recognized the knock and never knew if she was eager or angry when she heard it. And she didn't care.

When Violet came to visit (and Alice never knew when that might be) something opened up.

The dark hat made her face even darker. Her eyes were round as silver dollars but could slit of a sudden too.

The thing was how Alice felt and talked in her company. Not like she did with other people. With Violent she was impolite. Sudden. Frugal. No apology or courtesy seemed required or necessary between them. But something else was—clarity, perhaps. The kind of clarity crazy people demand from the not-crazy.

Violet, her coat lining repaired too now, her cuffs secure, needed only to pay attention to her hose and hat to appear normal. Alice sighed a little sigh, amazed at herself as she opened the door to the only visitor she looked forward to.

"You look froze."

"Near bout," said Violet.

"March can put you in the sickbed."

"Be a pleasure," Violet answered. "All my troubles be over if I could get my body sick stead of my head."

"Then who would do the fancy women's hair?"

Violet laughed. "Nobody. Maybe nobody would do it and nobody would know the difference."

"The difference is more than a hairdo."

"They're just women, you know. Like us."

"No," said Alice. "No they're not. Not like me."

"I don't mean the trade. I mean the women."

"Oh, please," said Alice. "Let's get off that. I'm steeping you some tea."

"They were good to me when nobody else was. Me and Joe eat because of them."

"Don't tell me about it."

"Anytime I come close to borrowing or need extra, I can work all day any day on their heads."

"Don't tell me, I said. I don't want to hear about it and where their money comes from. You want tea or not?"

"Yeah. Okay. Why not? Why can't you hear about it?"

"Oh. The men. The nasty life. Don't they fight all the time? When you do their hair, you're not afraid they might start fighting?"

"Only when they sober." Violet smiled.

"Oh, well."

"They share men, fight them and fight over them, too."

"No woman should live like that."

"No. No woman should have to."

"Killing people." Alice sucked her teeth. "Makes me sick to my stomach." She poured the tea, then lifting cup and saucer, held it back while she looked at Violet.

"If you had found out about them before he killed her, would you have?"

"I wonder."

Alice handed her the tea. "I don't understand women like you. Women with knives." She snatched up a long-sleeved blouse and smoothed it over the ironing board.

"I wasn't born with a knife."

"No, but you picked one up."

"You never did?" Violet blew ripples into the tea.

"No, I never did. Even when my husband ran off I never did that. And you. You didn't even have a worthy enemy. Somebody worth killing. You picked up a knife to insult a dead girl."

"But that's better, ain't it? The harm was already done."

"She wasn't the enemy."

"Oh, yes she is. She's my enemy. Then, when I didn't know it, and now too."

"Why? Because she was young and pretty and took your husband away from you?"

Violet sipped her tea and did not answer. After a long silence, and after their talk had turned to trifles then on to the narrowness of life, Violet said to Alice Manfred, "Wouldn't you? You wouldn't fight for your man?"

Seeded in childhood, watered every day since, fear had sprouted through her veins all her life. Thinking war thoughts it had gathered, blossomed into another thing. Now, as she looked at this woman, Alice heard her question like the pop of a toy gun.

Somewhere in Springfield only the teeth were left. Maybe the skull, maybe not. If she dug down deep enough and tore off the top, she could be sure that the teeth would certainly be there. No lips to share with the woman she had shared them with. No fingers to lift her hips as he had lifted others. Just the teeth exposed now, nothing like the smile that had made her say, "Choose." And he did.

What she told Violet was true. She had never picked up a knife. What she neglected to say—what came flooding back to her now—was also true: every day and every night for seven months she, Alice Manfred, was starving for blood. Not his. Oh, no. For him she planned sugar in his motor, scissors to his tie, burned suits, slashed shoes, ripped socks. Vicious, childish acts of violence to inconvenience him, remind him. But no blood. Her craving settled on the red liquid coursing through the other woman's veins. An ice pick stuck in and pulled up would get it. Would a clothesline rope circling her neck and yanked with all Alice's strength make her spit it up? Her favorite, however, the dream that plumped her pillow at night, was seeing herself mount a horse, then ride it and find the woman alone on a road and gallop till she ran her down under four iron hooves; then back again, and again until there was nothing left but tormented road dirt signaling where the hussy had been.

He had chosen; so would she. And maybe after galloping through seven months of nights on a horse she neither owned nor knew how to ride, over the twitching, pulpy body of a woman who wore white shoes in winter, laughed loud as a child, and who had never seen a marriage license—maybe she would have done something wild. But after seven months she had to choose something else. The suit, the tie, the shirt he liked best. They suggested she not waste the shoes. No one would see them. But socks? Surely he has to have socks? Of course, said the mortician. Socks, of course. And what difference did it make that one of the mourners was her sworn and hated enemy laying white roses on the coffin, taking away one the color of her dress. For thirty years he was turning into teeth in Springfield, and neither she nor the mourner in the inappropriate dress could do a thing about it.

Alice slammed the pressing iron down. "You don't know what loss is," she said, and listened as closely to what she was saying as did the woman sitting by her ironing board in a hat in the morning.

The hat, pushed back on her forehead, gave Violet a scatty look. The calming effect of the tea Alice Manfred had given her did not last long. Afterward she sat in the drugstore sucking malt through a straw wondering who on earth that other Violet was that walked about the City in her skin; peeped out through her eyes and saw other things. Where she saw a lonesome chair left like an orphan in a park strip facing the river that other Violet saw how the ice skim gave the railing's black poles a weapony glint. Where she, last in line at the car stop, noticed a child's cold wrist jutting out of a too-short, hand-me-down coat, *that* Violet slammed past a whitewoman into the seat of a trolley four minutes late. And if she turned away from faces looking past her through restaurant windows, *that* Violet heard the clack of the plate glass in mean March wind. She forgot which way to turn the key in the lock; *that* Violet not only knew the knife was in the parrot's cage and not in the kitchen drawer, *that* Violet remembered what she did not: scraping marble from the parrot's claws and beak weeks ago. She had been looking for that knife for a month. Couldn't for the life of her think what she'd done with it. But *that* Violet knew and went right to it. Knew too where the funeral was going on, although it could not have been but one of two places, come to think of it. Still, *that* Violet knew which of the two, and the right time to get there. Just before the closing of the casket, when the people who were going to faint fainted and the women in white dresses were fanning them. And the ushers, young men the same age as the deceased—from the dead girl's junior high school class, with freshly barbered heads and ghost-white gloves—gathered; first in a tight knot of six and then separated into two lines of three, they moved down the aisle from the back where they had assembled and surrounded the bier. They were the ones *that* Violet had to push aside, elbow her way into. And they did. Step aside, thinking maybe this was some last-minute love desperate to make itself known before it couldn't see and might forget the sleeping face it treasured. The ushers saw the knife before she did. Before she knew what was going on, the boy ushers' hard hands—knuckle-tough from marbles and steelies, from snowballs packed to bullet strength, from years of sticks sending hardballs over the hoods of motor cars, into lots with high fences and even into the open windows as well as the closed of people living four floors up, hands that had held the boys' whole body weight from the iron railings of El bridges—these hands were reaching toward the blade she had not seen for a month at least and was surprised to see now aimed at the girl's haughty, secret face.

It bounced off, making a little dent under her earlobe, like a fold in the skin that was hardly a disfigurement at all. She could have left it at that: the fold under the earlobe, but *that* Violet, unsatisfied, fought with the hard-handed usher boys and was time enough for them, almost. They had to forget right away that this was a fifty-year-old woman in a fur-collared coat and a hat pulled down so far over her right eye it was a wonder she saw the door to the church not to speak of the right place to aim her knife. They had to abandon the teachings they had had all their lives about the respect due their elders. Lessons learned from the old folks whose milky-light eyes watched everything they did, commented on it, and told each other what it was. Lessons they had learned from the younger old folks (like her) who could be their auntie, their grandmother, their mother, or their mother's best friend, who not only could tell on them, but could tell them; could stop them cold with a word, with a "Cut that mess out!" shouted from any window, doorway or street curb in a two-block radius. And they would cut it out, or take it downstairs behind the trunks, or off in a neglected park, or better still, in the shadow of the El where no lights lit what these women did not allow, don't care whose child it was. But they did it nevertheless. Forgot the lessons of a lifetime, and concentrated on the wide, shining blade, because who knew? Maybe she had more than one cutting in mind. Or maybe they could see themselves hangdog at the dinner table trying to explain to these same women or even, Jesus! the men, the fathers and uncles, and grown cousins, friends and neighbors, why they had just stood there like streetlights and let this woman in a fur-collared coat make fools of them and ruin the honorable job they had worn white gloves for. They had to wrestle her to the floor before she let go. And the sound that came from her mouth belonged to something wearing a pelt instead of a coat.

By then the usher boys were joined by frowning men, who carried *that* kicking, growling Violet out while she looked on in amazement. She had not been that strong since Virginia, since she loaded hay and handled the mule wagon like a full-grown man. But twenty years doing hair in the City had softened her arms and melted the shield that once covered her palms and fingers. Like shoes taking away the tough leather her bare feet had grown, the City took away the back and arm power she used to boast of. A power *that* Violet had not lost because she gave the usher boys, and the grown men too, a serious time.

*That* Violet should not have let the parrot go. He forgot how to fly and just trembled on the sill, but when she ran home from the funeral, having been literally thrown out by the hard-handed boys and the frowning men, "I love you" was exactly what neither she nor *that* Violet could bear to hear. She tried not to look at him as she paced the rooms, but the parrot saw her and squawked a weak "Love you" through the pane.

Joe, who had been missing since New Year's Day, did not come home that night or the next for her black-eyed peas. Gistan and Stuck came by to ask for him, to say they couldn't play cards Friday and to linger with embarrassment in the hall while Violet stared at them. So she knew the parrot was there because she kept going up and down the stairs from her apartment door to the front door to see if Joe was coming down the street. At two in the morning, again at four, she made the trip, peered out into the dark street, solitary except for a pair of police and cats peeing in the snow. The parrot, shivering and barely turning his green and blond head, told her each time, "Love you."

"Get away," she told him. "Go on off somewhere!"

The second morning he had. All she saw, down in the cellar well beneath the stoop, was a light yellow feather with a tip of green. And she had never named him. Had called him "my parrot" all these years. "My parrot." "Love you." "Love you." Did the dogs get him? Did some night-walking man snatch him up and take him to a house that did not feature mirrors or keep a supply of ginger cookies for him? Or did he get the message—that she said, "My parrot" and he said, "Love you," and she had never said it back or even taken the trouble to name him—and manage somehow to fly away on wings that had not soared for six years. Wings grown stiff from disuse and dull in the bulb light of an apartment with no view to speak of.

The malted was gone and although her stomach seemed about to lose its stitching, she ordered another and took it over behind the secondhand magazine rack to one of the little tables that Duggie had placed there against the law that said if he did it, it made the place a restaurant. There she could sit and watch the foam disappear, the scoops of ice cream lose their ridges and turn to soft, glistening balls like soap bars left in a dishpan full of water.

She had meant to bring a package of Dr. Dee's Nerve and Flesh Builder to stir into the malted milkshake, because the milkshakes alone didn't seem to be doing any good. The hips she came here with were gone, too, just like the power in her back and arms. Maybe *that* Violet, the one who knew where the butcher knife was and was strong enough to use it, had the hips she had lost. But if *that* Violet was strong and had hips, why was she proud of trying to kill a dead girl, and she was proud. Whenever she thought about *that* Violet, and what *that* Violet saw through her own eyes, she knew there was no shame there, no disgust. That was hers alone, so she hid behind the rack at one of Duggie's little illegal tables and played with the straw in a chocolate malt. She could have been eighteen herself, just like the girl at the magazine rack, reading *Collier's* and playing for time in the drugstore. Did Dorcas, when she was alive, like *Collier's? Liberty Magazine?* Did the blonde ladies with shingled hair capture her? Did the men in golf shoes and V-neck sweaters? How could they if she found herself stuck on a man old enough to be her father? A man who carried not a golf club but a sample case of Cleopatra products. A man whose handkerchiefs were not lightweight cotton poking from his jacket pocket, but red and large and spotted with white dots. Did he ask her to warm with her own body his spot in the bed on cold winter nights before he slid in? Or did he do it for her? He probably let her put her spoon into his pint of cream and scoop off the melty part, and when they sat in the dark of the Lincoln Theater he wouldn't mind a bit if she stuck her hand down in his box of popcorn and came up with a fistful of it the sonofabitch. And when "Wings Over Jordan" came on he probably turned the volume down so he could hear her when she sang along with the choir, instead of up so as to drown out her rendition of "Lay my body down." Turned, too, his jaw to the light of the bulb so she could press out between her thumbnails the hair root caught in a pore the dog. And another damn thing. (The malt was soup now, smooth and cold.) The twenty-five-dollar bonus prize of a blue-shaded boudoir lamp or an orchid-colored satinlike ladies' robe that he won and was due to him for having sold all that merchandise in one month—did he give that to her the heifer? Take her to Indigo on Saturday and sit way back so they could hear the music wide and be in the dark at the same time, at one of those round tables with a slick black top and a tablecloth of pure white on it, drinking rough gin with that sweet red stuff in it so it looked like soda pop, which a girl like her ought to have ordered instead of liquor she could sip from the edge of a glass wider at the mouth than at its base, with a tiny stem like a flower in between while her hand, the one that wasn't holding the glass shaped like a flower, was under the table drumming out the rhythm on the inside of his thigh, his thigh, his thigh, thigh, thigh, and he bought her underwear with stitching done to look like rosebuds and violets, VIOLETS, don't you know, and she wore it for him thin as it was and too cold for a room that couldn't count on a radiator to work through the afternoon, while I was where? Sliding on ice trying to get to somebody's kitchen to do their hair? Huddled in a doorway out of the wind waiting for the trolley? Wherever it was, it was cold and I was cold and nobody had got into the bed sheets early to warm up a spot for me or reached around my shoulders to pull the quilt up under my neck or even my ears because it got that cold sometimes it did and maybe that is why the butcher knife struck the neckline just by the earlobe. That's why. And that's why it took so much wrestling to get me down, keep me down and out of that coffin where she was the heifer who took what was mine, what I chose, picked out and determined to have and hold on to, NO! *that* Violet is not somebody walking round town, up and down the streets wearing my skin and using my eyes shit no *that* Violet is me! The me that hauled hay in Virginia and handled a four-mule team in the brace. I have stood in cane fields in the middle of the night when the sound of it rustling hid the slither of the snakes and I stood still waiting for him and not stirring a speck in case he was near and I would miss him, and damn the snakes my man was coming for me and who or what was going to keep me from him? Plenty times, plenty times I have carried the welts given me by a two-tone peckerwood because I was late in the field row the next morning. Plenty times, plenty, I chopped twice the wood that was needed into short logs and kindlin so as to make sure the crackers had enough and wouldn't go hollering for me when I was bound to meet my Joe Trace don't care what, and do what you will or may he was my Joe Trace. Mine. I picked him out from all the others wasn't nobody like Joe he make anybody stand in cane in the middle of the night; make any woman dream about him in the daytime so hard she miss the rut and have to work hard to get the mules back on the track. Any woman, not just me. Maybe that is what she saw. Not the fifty-year-old man toting a sample case, but my Joe Trace, my Virginia Joe Trace who carried a light inside him, whose shoulders were razor sharp and who looked at me with two-color eyes and never saw anybody else. Could she have looked at him and seen that? Under the table at the Indigo was she drumming on a thigh soft as a baby's but feeling all the while the way it used to be skin so tight it almost split and let the iron muscle through? Did she feel that, know that? That and other things, things I should have known and didn't? Secret things kept hidden from me or things I didn't notice? Is that why he let her scoop the melty part from around the edges of his pint of ice cream, stick her hand down in his salt-and-butter popcorn.

What did she see, young girl like that, barely out of high school, with unbraided hair, lip rouge for the first time and high-heeled shoes? And also what did he? A young me with high-yellow skin instead of black? A young me with long wavy hair instead of short? Or a not me at all. A me he was loving in Virginia because that girl Dorcas wasn't around there anywhere. Was that it? Who was it? Who was he thinking of when he ran in the dark to meet me in the cane field? Somebody golden, like my own golden boy, who I never ever saw but who tore up my girlhood as surely as if we'd been the best of lovers? Help me God help me if that was it, because I knew him and loved him better than anybody except True Belle who is the one made me crazy about him in the first place. Is that what happened? Standing in the cane, he was trying to catch a girl he was yet to see, but his heart knew all about, and me, holding on to him but wishing he was the golden boy I never saw either. Which means from the very beginning I was a substitute and so was he.

I got quiet because the things I couldn't say were coming out of my mouth anyhow. I got quiet because I didn't know what my hands might get up to when the day's work was done. The business going on inside me I thought was none of my business and none of Joe's either because I just had to keep hold of him any way I could and going crazy would make me lose him.

Sitting in the thin sharp light of the drugstore playing with a long spoon in a tall glass made her think of another woman occupying herself at a table pretending to drink from a cup. Her mother. She didn't want to be like that. Oh never like that. To sit at the table, alone in the moonlight, sipping boiled coffee from a white china cup as long as it was there, and pretending to sip it when it was gone; waiting for morning when men came, talking low as though nobody was there but themselves, and picked around in our things, lifting out what they wanted—what was theirs, they said, although we cooked in it, washed sheets in it, sat on it, ate off of it. That was after they had hauled away the plow, the scythe, the mule, the sow, the churn and the butter press. Then they came inside the house and all of us children put one foot on the other and watched. When they got to the table where our mother sat nursing an empty cup, they took the table out from under her and then, while she sat there alone, and all by herself like, cup in hand, they came back and tipped the chair she sat in. She didn't jump up right away, so they shook it a bit and since she still stayed seated—looking ahead at nobody—they just tipped her out of it like the way you get the cat off the seat if you don't want to touch it or pick it up in your arms. You tip it forward and it lands on the floor. No harm done if it's a cat because it has four legs. But a person, a woman, might fall forward and just stay there a minute looking at the cup, stronger than she is, unbroken at least and lying a bit beyond her hand. Just out of reach.

There were five of them, Violet the third, and they all came in the house finally and said mama; each one came and said it until she said uh huh. They never heard her say anything else in the days that followed, when, huddled in an abandoned shack, they were thoroughly dependent upon the few neighbors left in 1888—the ones who had not moved west to Kansas City or Oklahoma; north to Chicago or Bloomington Indiana. It was through one of the last-to-leave families, bound for Philadelphia, that the message of Rose Dear's distress reached True Belle. Those who stayed brought things: a pallet, a pot, some pan bread and a bucket of milk. Advice too: "Don't let this whip you, Rose. You got us, Rose Dear. Think of the young ones, Rose. He ain't give you nothing you can't bear, Rose." But had He? Maybe this one time He had. Had misjudged and misunderstood her particular backbone. This one time. This here particular spine.

Rose's mother, True Belle, came when she heard. Left her cushiony job in Baltimore and, with ten eagle dollars stitched separately into her skirts to keep them quiet, came back to a little depot called Rome in Vesper County to take charge and over. The little girls fell in love right away and things got put back together. Slowly but steadily, for about four years, True Belle got things organized. And then Rose Dear jumped in the well and missed all the fun. Two weeks after her burial, Rose's husband arrived loaded with ingots of gold for the children, two-dollar pieces for the women and snake oil for the men. For Rose Dear he brought a silk embroidered pillow to comfort her back on a sofa nobody ever had, but would have been real nice under her head in the pine box—if only he'd been on time. The children ate the chocolate from the ingots of gold and traded the heavenly paper among themselves for reed whistles and fishing string. The women bit the piece of silver before knotting it tightly in their clothes. Except True Belle. She fingered the money and, looking back and forth from the coin to her son-in-law, shook her head and laughed.

"Damn," he said. "Aw, damn," when he heard what Rose had done.

Twenty-one days later he was gone again, and Violet was married to Joe and living in the City when she heard from a sister that he'd done it again: arrived in Rome with treasures weighing his pockets and folded under the cap on his head. His trips back were both bold and secret for he had been mixed in and up with the Readjuster Party, and when a verbal urging from landowners had not worked, a physical one did the trick and he was persuaded to transfer hisself someplace, anyplace, else. Perhaps he planned to find some way to get them all out; in the meantime he made fabulously dangerous and wonderful returns over the years, although the interims got longer and longer, and while the likelihood that he was still alive grew fainter, hope never did. Anytime anytime, on another brittle cold Monday or in the blasting heat of a Sunday night, he might be there, owl-whistling from the road, the mocking, daring dollar bills sticking from his cap, jammed into the cuffs of his trousers and the tops of his shoes. Candy stuck in clumps in his coat pocket along with a tin of Frieda's Egyptian Hair Pomade. Bottles of rye, purgative waters and eaux for every conceivable toilette made a companionable click in his worn carpet bag.

He'd be in his seventies now. Slower for sure, and maybe he'd lost the teeth that made the smile that made the sisters forgive him. But for Violet (as well as for her sisters and those who stayed in the county) he was out there somewhere gathering and putting by delights to pass out among the homefolks. For who could keep him down, this defiant birthday-every-day man who dispensed gifts and stories that kept them so rapt they forgot for the while a bone-clean cupboard and exhausted soil; or believed a child's leg would straighten itself out by and by. Forgot why he left in the first place and was forced to sneak into his own home ground. In his company forgetfulness fell like pollen. But for Violet the pollen never blotted out Rose. In the midst of the joyful resurrection of this phantom father, taking pleasure in the distribution of his bounty both genuine and fake, Violet never forgot Rose Dear or the place she had thrown herself into—a place so narrow, so dark it was pure, breathing relief to see her stretched in a wooden box.

"Thank God for life," True Belle said, "and thank life for death."

Rose. Dear Rose Dear.

What was the thing, I wonder, the one and final thing she had not been able to endure or repeat? Had the last washing split the shirtwaist so bad it could not take another mend and changed its name to rag? Perhaps word had reached her about the four-day hangings in Rocky Mount: the men on Tuesday, the women two days later. Or had it been the news of the young tenor in the choir mutilated and tied to a log, his grandmother refusing to give up his waste-filled trousers, washing them over and over although the stain had disappeared at the third rinse. They buried him in his brother's pants and the old woman pumped another bucket of clear water. Might it have been the morning after the night when craving (which used to be hope) got out of hand? When longing squeezed, then tossed her before running off promising to return and bounce her again like an India-rubber ball? Or was it that chair they tipped her out of? Did she fall on the floor and lie there deciding right then that she would do it. Someday. Delaying it for four years while True Belle came and took over but remembering the floorboards as a door, closed and locked. Seeing bleak truth in an unbreakable china cup? Biding her time until the moment returned—with all its mewing hurt or overboard rage—and she could turn away from the door, the cup to step toward the limitlessness beckoning from the well. What could it have been, I wonder?

True Belle was there, chuckling, competent, stitching by firelight, gardening and harvesting by day. Pouring mustard tea on the girls' cuts and bruises, and keeping them at their tasks with spellbinding tales of her Baltimore days and the child she had cared for there. Maybe it was that: knowing her daughters were in good hands, better hands than her own, at last, and Rose Dear was free of time that no longer flowed, but stood stock-still when they tipped her from her kitchen chair. So she dropped herself down the well and missed all the fun.

The important thing, the biggest thing Violet got out of that was to never never have children. Whatever happened, no small dark foot would rest on another while a hungry mouth said, Mama?

As she grew older, Violet could neither stay where she was nor go away. The well sucked her sleep, but the notion of leaving frightened her. It was True Belle who forced it. There were bully cotton crops in Palestine and people for twenty miles around were going to pick it. Rumor was the pay was ten cents for young women, a quarter for men. Three double seasons in a row of bad weather had ruined all expectations and then came the day when the blossoms jumped out fat and creamy. Everybody held his breath while the landowner squinted his eyes and spat. His two black laborers walked the rows, touching the tender flowers, fingering the soil and trying to puzzle out the sky. Then one day of light, fresh rain, four dry, hot and clear, and all of Palestine was downy with the cleanest cotton they'd ever seen. Softer than silk, and out so fast the weevils, having abandoned the fields years ago, had no time to get back there.

Three weeks. It all had to be done in three weeks or less. Everybody with fingers in a twenty-mile radius showed up and was hired on the spot. Nine dollars a bale, some said, if you grew your own; eleven dollars if you had a white friend to carry it up for pricing. And for pickers, ten cents a day for the women and a case quarter for the men.

True Belle sent Violet and two of her sisters in the fourth wagonload to go. They rode all night, assembled at dawn, ate what was handed out and shared the meadows and the stars with local people who saw no point in going all the way home for five hours' sleep.

Violet had no talent for it. She was seventeen years old but trailed with the twelve-year-olds—making up the last in line or meeting the others on their way back down the row. For this she was put to scragging, second-picking the bushes that had a few inferior puffs left on the twigs by swifter hands than hers. Humiliated, teased to tears, she had about decided to beg a way back to Rome when a man fell out of the tree above her head and landed at her side. She had lain down one night, sulking and abashed, a little way from her sisters, but not too far. Not too far to crawl back to them swiftly if the trees turned out to be full of spirits idling the night away. The spot she had chosen to spread her blanket was under a handsome black walnut that grew at the edge of the woods bordering the acres of cotton.

The thump could not have been a raccoon's because it said Ow. Violet rolled away too scared to speak, but raised on all fours to dash.

"Never happened before," said the man. "I've been sleeping up there every night. This the first time I fell out."

Violet could see his outline in a sitting position and that he was rubbing his arm then his head then his arm again.

"You sleep in trees?"

"If I find me a good one."

"Nobody sleeps in trees."

"I sleep in them."

"Sounds softheaded to me. Could be snakes up there."

"Snakes around here crawl the ground at night. Now who's softheaded?"

"Could've killed me."

"Might still, if my arm ain't broke."

"I hope it is. You won't be picking nothing in the morning and climbing people's trees either."

"I don't pick cotton. I work the gin house."

"What you doing out here, then, Mr. High and Mighty, sleeping in trees like a bat?"

"You don't have one nice word for a hurt man?"

"Yeah: find somebody else's tree."

"You act like you own it."

"You act like you do."

"Say we share it."

"Not me."

He stood up and shook his leg before trying his weight on it, then limped toward the tree.

"You not going back up there over my head."

"Get my tarp," he said. "Rope broke. That's what did it." He scanned the night for the far reaches of the branches. "See it? There it is. Hanging right there. Yep." He sat down then, his back resting on the trunk. "Have to wait till it's light, though," he said and Violet always believed that because their first conversation began in the dark (when neither could see much more of the other than silhouette) and ended in a green-and-white dawn, nighttime was never the same for her. Never again would she wake struggling against the pull of a narrow well. Or watch first light with the sadness left over from finding Rose Dear in the morning twisted into water much too small.

His name was Joseph, and even before the sun rose, when

it was still hidden in the woods, but freshening the world's green and dazzling acres of white cotton against the gash of a ruby horizon, Violet claimed him. Hadn't he fallen practically in her lap? Hadn't he stayed? All through the night, taking her sass, complaining, teasing, explaining, but talking, talking her through the dark. And with daylight came the bits of him: his smile and his wide watching eyes. His buttonless shirt open to a knot at the waist exposed a chest she claimed as her own smooth pillow. The shaft of his legs, the plane of his shoulders, jawline and long fingers—she claimed it all. She knew she must be staring, and tried to look away, but the contrasting color of his two eyes brought her glance back each and every time. She grew anxious when she heard workers begin to stir, anticipating the breakfast call, going off in the trees to relieve themselves, muttering morning sounds—but then he said, "I'll be back in our tree tonight. Where you be?"

"Under it," she said and rose from the clover like a woman with important things to do.

She did not worry what could happen in three weeks when she was supposed to take her two dollars and ten cents back to True Belle. As it turned out, she sent it back with her sisters and stayed in the vicinity hunting work. The straw boss had no faith in her, having watched her sweating hard to fill her sack as quickly as the children, but she was highly and suddenly vocal in her determination.

She moved in with a family of six in Tyrell and worked at anything to be with Joe whenever she could. It was there she became the powerfully strong young woman who could handle mules, bale hay and chop wood as good as any man. It was there where the palms of her hands and the soles of her feet grew shields no gloves or shoes could match. All for Joe Trace, a double-eyed nineteen-year-old who lived with an adopted family, worked gins and lumber and cane and cotton and corn, who butchered when needed, plowed, fished, sold skins and game—and who was willing. He loved the woods. Loved them. So it was shocking to his family and friends not when he agreed to marry Violet, but that, thirteen years later, he agreed to take her to Baltimore, where she said all the houses had separate rooms and water came to you—not you to it. Where colored men worked harbors for $2.50 a day, pulling cargo from ships bigger than churches, and others drove up to the very door of your house to take you where you needed to be. She was describing a Baltimore of twenty-five years ago and a neighborhood neither she nor Joe could rent in, but she didn't know that, and never knew it, because they went to the City instead. Their Baltimore dreams were displaced by more powerful ones. Joe knew people living in the City and some who'd been there and come home with tales to make Baltimore weep. The money to be earned for doing light work—standing in front of a door, carrying food on a tray, even cleaning strangers' shoes—got you in a day more money than any of them had earned in one whole harvest. Whitepeople literally threw money at you—just for being neighborly: opening a taxi door, picking up a package. And anything you had or made or found you could sell in the streets. In fact, there were streets where colored people owned all the stores; whole blocks of handsome colored men and women laughing all night and making money all day. Steel cars sped down the streets and if you saved up, they said, you could get you one and drive as long as there was road.

For fourteen years Joe listened to these stories and laughed. But he resisted them too, until, abruptly, he changed his mind. No one, not even Violet, knew what it was that permitted him to leave his fields and woods and secret lonely valleys. To give away his fishing pole, his skinning knife—every piece of his gear but one, and borrow a suitcase for their things. Violet never knew what it was that fired him up and made him want—all of a sudden, but later than most—to move to the City. She supposed that the dinner that tickled everybody must have played a part in Joe's change of mind. If Booker T. was sitting down to eat a chicken sandwich in the President's house in a city called capital, near where True Belle had had such a good time, then things must be all right, all right. He took his bride on a train ride electric enough to pop their eyes and danced on into the City.

Violet thought it would disappoint them; that it would be less lovely than Baltimore. Joe believed it would be perfect. When they arrived, carrying all of their belongings in one valise, they both knew right away that perfect was not the word. It was better than that.

Joe didn't want babies either so all those miscarriages—two in the field, only one in her bed—were more inconvenience than loss. And citylife would be so much better without them. Arriving at the train station back in 1906, the smiles they both smiled at the women with little children, strung like beads over suitcases, were touched with pity. They liked children. Loved them even. Especially Joe, who had a way with them. But neither wanted the trouble. Years later, however, when Violet was forty, she was already staring at infants, hesitating in front of toys displayed at Christmas. Quick to anger when a sharp word was flung at a child, or a woman's hold of a baby seemed awkward or careless. The worst burn she ever made was on the temple of a customer holding a child across her knees. Violet, lost in the woman's hand-patting and her knee-rocking the little boy, forgot her own hand holding the curling iron. The customer flinched and the skin discolored right away. Violet moaned her apologies and the woman was satisfied until she discovered that the whole curl was singed clean off. Skin healed, but an empty spot in her hairline . . . Violet had to forgo payment to shut her up.

By and by longing became heavier than sex: a panting, unmanageable craving. She was limp in its thrall or rigid in an effort to dismiss it. That was when she bought herself a present; hid it under the bed to take out in secret when it couldn't be helped. She began to imagine how old that last miscarried child would be now. A girl, probably. Certainly a girl. Who would she favor? What would her speaking voice sound like? After weaning time, Violet would blow her breath on the babygirl's food, cooling it down for the tender mouth. Later on they would sing together, Violet taking the alto line, the girl a honeyed soprano. "Don't you remember, a long time ago, two little babes their names I don't know, carried away one bright summer's day, lost in the woods I hear people say that the sun went down and the stars shone their light. Poor babes in the woods they laid down and died. When they were dead a robin so red put strawberry leaves over their heads." Aw. Aw. Later on Violet would dress her hair for her the way the girls wore it now: short, bangs paper sharp above the eyebrows? Ear curls? Razor-thin part on the side? Hair sliding into careful waves marcelled to a T?

Violet was drowning in it, deep-dreaming. Just when her breasts were finally flat enough not to need the binders the young women wore to sport the chest of a soft boy, just when her nipples had lost their point, mother-hunger had hit her like a hammer. Knocked her down and out. When she woke up, her husband had shot a girl young enough to be that daughter whose hair she had dressed to kill. Who lay there asleep in that coffin? Who posed there awake in the photograph? The scheming bitch who had not considered Violet's feelings one tiniest bit, who came into a life, took what she wanted and damn the consequences? Or mama's dumpling girl? Was she the woman who took the man, or the daughter who fled her womb? Washed away on a tide of soap, salt and castor oil. Terrified, perhaps, of so violent a home. Unaware that, had it failed, had she braved mammymade poisons and mammy's urgent fists, she could have had the best-dressed hair in the City. Instead, she hung around in the fat knees of strangers' children. In shop windows, and baby carriages left for a moment in the sun. Not realizing that, bitch or dumpling, the two of them, mother and daughter, could have walked Broadway together and ogled the clothes. Could be sitting together, cozy in the kitchen, while Violet did her hair.

"Another time," she said to Alice Manfred, "another time I would have loved her too. Just like you did. Just like Joe." She was holding her coat lapels closed, too embarrassed to let her hostess hang it up lest she see the lining.

"Maybe," said Alice. "Maybe. You'll never know now, though, will you?"

"I thought she was going to be pretty. Real pretty. She wasn't."

"Pretty enough, I'd say."

"You mean the hair. The skin color."

"Don't tell me what I mean."

"Then what? What he see in her?"

"Shame on you. Grown woman like you asking me that."

"I have to know."

"Then ask the one who does know. You see him every day."

"Don't get mad."

"Will if I want to."

"All right. But I don't want to ask him. I don't want to hear what he has to say about it. You know what I'm asking."

"Forgiveness is what you're asking and I can't give you that. It's not in my power."

"No, not that. That's not it, forgiveness."

"What, then? Don't get pitiful. I won't stand for you getting pitiful, hear me?"

"We born around the same time, me and you," said Violet. "We women, me and you. Tell me something real. Don't just say I'm grown and ought to know. I don't. I'm fifty and I don't know nothing. What about it? Do I stay with him? I want to, I think. I want . . . well, I didn't always . . . now I want. I want some fat in this life."

"Wake up. Fat or lean, you got just one. This is it."

"You don't know either, do you?"

"I know enough to know how to behave."

"Is that it? Is that all it is?"

"Is that all what is?"

"Oh shoot! Where the grown people? Is it us?"

"Oh, Mama." Alice Manfred blurted it out and then covered her mouth.

Violet had the same thought: Mama. Mama? Is this where you got to and couldn't do it no more? The place of shade without trees where you know you are not and never again will be loved by anybody who can choose to do it? Where everything is over but the talking?

They looked away from each other then. The silence went on and on until Alice Manfred said, "Give me that coat. I can't look at that lining another minute."

Violet stood up and took off her coat, carefully pulling her arms trapped in frayed silk. Then she sat down and watched the seamstress go to work.

"All I could think of was to step out on him like he did me."

"Fool," said Alice and broke the thread.

"Couldn't name him if my life depended on it."

"Bet he can name you."

"Let him."

"What did you think that was going to solve?"

Violet didn't answer.

"Did it get you your husband's attention?"

"No."

"Open my niece's grave?"

"No."

"Do I have to say it again?"

"Fool? No. No, but tell me, I mean, listen. Everybody I grew up with is down home. We don't have children. He's what I got. He's what I got."

"Doesn't look so," said Alice. Her stitches were invisible to the eye.

Late in March, sitting in Duggie's drugstore, Violet played with a spoon, recalling the visit she had paid to Alice that morning. She had come early. Chore time and Violet wasn't doing any.

"It's different from what I thought," she said. "Different."

Violet meant twenty years of life in a City better than perfect, but Alice did not ask her what she meant. Did not ask her whether the City, with its streets all laid out, aroused jealousy too late for anything but foolishness. Or if it was the City that produced a crooked kind of mourning for a rival young enough to be a daughter.

They had been talking about prostitutes and fighting

women—Alice nettled; Violet indifferent. Then silence while Violet drank tea and listened to the hissing iron. By this time the women had become so easy with each other talk wasn't always necessary. Alice ironed and Violet watched. From time to time one murmured something—to herself or to the other.

"I used to love that stuff," said Violet.

Alice smiled, knowing without looking up that Violet meant the starch. "Me too," she said. "Drove my husband crazy."

"Is it the crunch? Couldn't be the taste."

Alice shrugged. "Only the body knows."

The iron hissed at the damp fabric. Violet leaned her cheek on her palm. "You iron like my grandmother. Yoke last."

"That's the test of a first-class ironing."

"Some do it yoke first."

"And have to do it over. I hate a lazy ironing."

"Where you learn to sew like that?"

"They kept us children busy. Idle hands, you know."

"We picked cotton, chopped wood, plowed. I never knew what it was to fold my hands. This here is as close as I ever been to watching my hands do nothing."

Eating starch, choosing when to tackle the yoke, sewing, picking, cooking, chopping. Violet thought about it all and sighed. "I thought it would be bigger than this. I knew it wouldn't last, but I did think it'd be bigger."

Alice refolded the cloth around the handle of the pressing iron. "He'll do it again, you know. And again and again and again."

"In that case I'd better throw him out now."

"Then what?"

Violet shook her head. "Watch the floorboards, I guess."

"You want a real thing?" asked Alice. "I'll tell you a real one. You got anything left to you to love, anything at all, do it."

Violet raised her head. "And when he does it again? Don't mind what people think?"

"Mind what's left to you."

"You saying take it? Don't fight?"

Alice put down her iron, hard. "Fight what, who? Some mishandled child who saw her parents burn up? Who knew better than you or me or anybody just how small and quick this little bitty life is? Or maybe you want to stomp somebody with three kids and one pair of shoes. Somebody in a raggedy dress, the hem dragging in the mud. Somebody wanting arms just like you do and you want to go over there and hold her but her dress is muddy at the hem and the people standing around wouldn't understand how could anybody's eyes go so flat, how could they? Nobody's asking you to take it. I'm sayin make it, make it!"

It took her a moment to notice that Violet was staring. Following her gaze Alice lifted the iron and saw what Violet saw: the black and smoking ship burned clear through the yoke.

"Shit!" Alice shouted. "Oh, shit!"

Violet was the first to smile. Then Alice. In no time laughter was rocking them both. Violet was reminded of True Belle, who entered the single room of their cabin and laughed to beat the band. They were hunched like mice near a can fire, not even a stove, on the floor, hungry and irritable. True Belle looked at them and had to lean against the wall to keep her laughter from pulling her down to the floor with them. They should have hated her. Gotten up from the floor and hated her. But what they felt was better. Not beaten, not lost. Better. They laughed too, even Rose Dear shook her head and smiled, and suddenly the world was right side up. Violet learned then what she had forgotten until this moment: that laughter is serious. More complicated, more serious than tears.

Crumpled over, shoulders shaking, Violet thought about how she must have looked at the funeral, at what her mission was. The sight of herself trying to do something bluesy, something hep, fumbling the knife, too late anyway . . . She laughed till she coughed and Alice had to make them both a cup of settling tea.

Committed as Violet was to hip development, even she couldn't drink the remaining malt—watery, warm and flat-tasting. She buttoned her coat and left the drugstore and noticed, at the same moment as *that* Violet did, that it was spring. In the City.

And when spring comes to the City people notice one another in the road; notice the strangers with whom they share aisles and tables and the space where intimate garments are laundered. Going in and out, in and out the same door, they handle the handle; on trolleys and park benches they settle thighs on a seat in which hundreds have done it too. Copper coins dropped in the palm have been swallowed by children and tested by gypsies, but it's still money and people smile at that. It's the time of year when the City urges contradiction most, encouraging you to buy street food when you have no appetite at all; giving you a taste for a single room occupied by you alone as well as a craving to share it with someone you passed in the street. Really there is no contradiction—rather it's a condition: the range of what an artful City can do. What can beat bricks warming up to the sun? The return of awnings. The removal of blankets from horses' backs. Tar softens under the heel and the darkness under bridges changes from gloom to cooling shade. After a light rain, when the leaves have come, tree limbs are like wet fingers playing in woolly green hair. Motor cars become black jet boxes gliding behind hoodlights weakened by mist. On sidewalks turned to satin figures move shoulder first, the crowns of their heads angled shields against the light buckshot that the raindrops are. The faces of children glimpsed at windows appear to be crying, but it is the glass pane dripping that makes it seem so.

In the spring of 1926, on a rainy afternoon, anybody passing through the alley next to a certain apartment house on Lenox might have looked up and seen, not a child but a grown man's face crying along with the glass pane. A strange sight you hardly ever see: men crying so openly. It's not a thing they do. Strange as it was, people finally got used to him, wiping his face and nose with an engineer's red handkerchief while he sat month after month by the window without view or on the stoop, first in the snow and later in the sun. I'd say Violet washed and ironed those handkerchiefs because, crazy as she was, raggedy as she became, she couldn't abide dirty laundry. But it tired everybody out waiting to see what else Violet would do besides try to kill a dead girl and keep her husband in tidy handkerchiefs. My own opinion was that one day she would stack up those handkerchiefs, take them to the dresser drawer, tuck them in and then go light his hair with a matchstick. She didn't but maybe that would have been better than what she did do. Meaning to or not meaning to, she got him to go through it again—at springtime when it's clearer then than as at no other time that citylife is streetlife.

Blind men thrum and hum in the soft air as they inch steadily down the walk. They don't want to stand near and compete with the old uncles positioning themselves in the middle of the block to play a six-string guitar.

Blues man. Black and bluesman. Blacktherefore blue man.

Everybody knows your name.

Where-did-she-go-and-why man. So-lonesome-I-could-die man.

Everybody knows your name.

The singer is hard to miss, sitting as he does on a fruit crate in the center of the sidewalk. His peg leg is stretched out comfy; his real one is carrying both the beat and the guitar's weight. Joe probably thinks that the song is about him. He'd like believing it. I know him so well. Have seen him feed small animals nobody else paid any attention to, but I was never deceived. I remember the way he used to fix his hat when he left the apartment building; how he moved it forward and a bit to the left. Whether stooping to remove a pile of horse flop or sauntering off to his swank hotel, his hat had to be just so. Not a tilt exactly, but a definite slant, you could say. The sweater under his suit jacket would be buttoned all the way up, but I know his thoughts are not—they are loose. He cuts his eyes over to the sweetbacks lounging on the corner. There is something they have he wants. Very little in his case of Cleopatra is something men would want to buy—except for aftershave dusting powder, most of it is for women. Women he can get to talk to, look at, flirt with and who knows what else is on his mind? And if she gives him more than the time of day with a look, the watching eyes of the sweetbacks are more satisfying than hers.

Or else he feels sorry about himself for being faithful in the first place. And if that virtue is unappreciated, and nobody jumps up to congratulate him on it, his self-pity turns to resentment which he has trouble understanding but no trouble focusing on the young sheiks, radiant and brutal, standing on street corners. Look out. Look out for a faithful man near fifty. Because he has never messed with another woman; because he selected that young girl to love, he thinks he is free. Not free to break loaves or feed the world on a fish. Nor to raise the war dead, but free to do something wild.

Take my word for it, he is bound to the track. It pulls him like a needle through the groove of a Bluebird record. Round and round about the town. That's the way the City spins you. Makes you do what it wants, go where the laid-out roads say to. All the while letting you think you're free; that you can jump into thickets because you feel like it. There are no thickets here and if mowed grass is okay to walk on the City will let you know. You can't get off the track a City lays for you. Whatever happens, whether you get rich or stay poor, ruin your health or live to old age, you always end up back where you started: hungry for the one thing everybody loses—young loving.

That was Dorcas, all right. Young but wise. She was Joe's personal sweet—like candy. It was the best thing, if you were young and had just got to the City. That and the clarinets and even they were called licorice sticks. But Joe has been in the City twenty years and isn't young anymore. I imagine him as one of those men who stop somewhere around sixteen. Inside.

So even though he wears button-up-the-front sweaters and round-toed shoes, he's a kid, a strapling, and candy could still make him smile. He likes those peppermint things last the live-long day, and thinks everybody else does too. Passes them out to Gistan's boys clowning on the curb. You could tell they'd rather chocolate or something with peanuts.

Makes me wonder about Joe. All those good things he gets from the Windemere, and he pays almost as much money for stale and sticky peppermint as he does for the room he rents to fuck in. Where his private candy box opens for him.

Rat. No wonder it ended the way it did. But it didn't have to, and if he had stopped trailing that little fast thing all over town long enough to tell Stuck or Gistan or some neighbor who might be interested, who knows how it would go?

"It's not a thing you tell to another man. I know most men can't wait to tell each other about what they got going on the side. Put all their business in the street. They do it because the woman don't matter all that much and they don't care what folks think about her. The most I did was halfway tell Malvonne and there was no way not to. But tell another man? No. Anyhow Gistan would just laugh and try to get out of hearing it. Stuck would look at his feet, swear I'd been fixed and tell me how much high john I need to remedy myself. Neither one of them I'd talk to about her. It's not a thing you tell except maybe to a tight friend, somebody you knew from before, long time ago like Victory, but even if I had the chance I don't believe I could have told him and if I couldn't tell Victory it was because I couldn't tell myself because I didn't know all about it. All I know is I saw her buying candy and the whole thing was sweet. Not just the candy—the whole thing and picture of it. Candy's something you lick, suck on, and then swallow and it's gone. No. This was something else. More like blue water and white flowers, and sugar in the air. I needed to be there, where it was all mixed up together just right, and where that was, was Dorcas.

"When I got to the apartment I had no name to put to the face I'd seen in the drugstore, and her face wasn't on my mind right then. But she opened the door, opened it right up to me. I smelled pound cake and disguised chicken. The women gathered around and I showed them what I had while they laughed and did the things women do: flicked lint off my jacket, pressed me on the shoulder to make me sit down. It's a way they have of mending you, fixing what they think needs repair.

"She didn't give me a look or say anything. But I knew where she was standing and how, every minute. She leaned her hip on the back of a chair in the parlor, while the women streamed out of the dining room to mend me and joke me. Then somebody called out her name. Dorcas. I didn't hear much else, but I stayed there and showed them all my stuff, smiling, not selling but letting them sell themselves.

"I sell trust; I make things easy. That's the best way. Never push. Like at the Windemere when I wait tables. I'm there but only if you want me. Or when I work the rooms, bringing up the whiskey hidden so it looks like coffee. Just there when you need me and right on time. You get to know the woman who wants four glasses of something, but doesn't want to ask four times; so you wait till her glass is two-thirds down and fill it up again. That way, she's drinking one glass while he is buying four. The quiet money whispers twice: once when I slide it in my pocket; once when I slide it out.

"I was prepared to wait, to have her ignore me. I didn't have a plan and couldn't have carried it out if I did. I felt dizzy with a lightheadedness I thought came from the heavy lemon flavoring, the face powder and that light woman-sweat. Salty. Not bitter like a man's is. I don't know to this day what made me speak to her on the way out the door.

"I can conjure what people say. That I treated Violet like a piece of furniture you favor although it needed something every day to keep it steady and upright. I don't know. But since Victory, I never got too close to anybody. Gistan and Stuck, we close, but not like it is with somebody knew you from when you was born and you got to manhood at the same time. I would have told Victory how it was. Gistan, Stuck, whatever I said to them would be something near, but not the way it really was. I couldn't talk to anybody but Dorcas and I told her things I hadn't told myself. With her I was fresh, new again. Before I met her I'd changed into new seven times. The first time was when I named my own self, since nobody did it for me, since nobody knew what it could or should have been.

"I was born and raised in Vesper County, Virginia, in 1873. Little place called Vienna. Rhoda and Frank Williams took me in right away and raised me along with six of their own. Her last child was three months old when Mrs. Rhoda took me in, and me and him were closer than many brothers I've seen. Victory was his name. Victory Williams. Mrs. Rhoda named me Joseph after her father, but neither she nor Mr. Frank either thought to give me a last name. She never pretended I was her natural child. When she parceled out chores or favors she'd say, 'You are just like my own.' That 'like' I guess it was made me ask her—I don't believe I was three yet—where my real parents were. She looked down at me, over her shoulder, and gave me the sweetest smile, but sad someway, and told me, O honey, they disappeared without a trace. The way I heard it I understood her to mean the 'trace' they disappeared without was me.

"The first day I got to school I had to have two names. I told the teacher Joseph Trace. Victory turned his whole self around in the seat.

" 'Why you tell her that?' he asked me.

" 'I don't know,' I said. 'Cause.'

" 'Mama be mad. Pappy too.'

"We were outside in the school yard. It was nice, packed dirt but a lot of nails and things were in it. Both of us barefoot. I was struggling to pick a bit of glass from the sole of my foot, so I didn't have to look up at him. 'No they won't,' I said. 'Your mama ain't my mama.'

" 'If she ain't, who is?'

" 'Another woman. She be back. She coming back for me. My daddy too.' That was the first time I knew I thought that, or wished it.

"Victory said, 'They know where they left you. They come back to our place. Williams place is where they know you at.' He was trying to walk double-jointed like his sister. She was good at it and bragged so much Victory practiced every chance he got. I remember his shadow darting in the dirt in front of me. 'They know you at Williams place, Williams is what you ought to call yourself.'

"I said, 'They got to pick me out. From all of you all, they got to pick me. I'm Trace, what they went off without.'

" 'Ain't that a bitch?'

"Victory laughed at me and wrapped his arm around my neck wrassling me to the ground. I don't know what happened to the speck of glass. I never did get it out. And nobody came looking for me either. I never knew my own daddy. And my mother, well, I heard a woman in the hotel dining room say the confoundest thing. She was talking to two other women while I poured the coffee. 'I am bad for my children,' she said. 'I don't mean to be, but there is something in me that makes it so. I'm a good mother but they do better away from me; as long as they're by my side nothing good can come to them. The ones that leave seem to flower; the ones that stay have such a hard time. You can imagine how bad I feel knowing that, can't you?'

"I had to sneak a look at her. It took strength to say that. Admit that.

"The second change came when I was picked out and trained to be a man. To live independent and feed myself no matter what. I didn't miss having a daddy because first off there was Mr. Frank. Steady as a rock, and showed no difference among any of us children. But the big thing was, I was picked, Victory too, by the best man in Vesper County to go hunting with. Talk about proud-making. He was the best in the county and he picked me and Victory to teach and hunt with. He was so good they say he just carried the rifle for the hell of it because he knew way before what the prey would do, how to fool snakes, bend twigs and string to catch rabbits, groundhog; make a sound waterfowl couldn't resist. Whitefolks said he was a witch doctor, but they said that so they wouldn't have to say he was smart. A hunter's hunter, that's what he was. Smart as they come. Taught me two lessons I lived by all my life. One was the secret of kindness from whitepeople—they had to pity a thing before they could like it. The other—well, I forgot it.

"It was because of him, what I learned from him, made me

more comfortable in the woods than in a town. I'd get nervous if a fence or a rail was anywhere around. Folks thought I was the one to be counted on never to be able to stomach a city. Piled-up buildings? Cement paths? Me? Not me.

"Eighteen ninety-three was the third time I changed. That was when Vienna burned to the ground. Red fire doing fast what white sheets took too long to finish: canceling every deed; vacating each and every field; emptying us out of our places so fast we went running from one part of the county to another—or nowhere. I walked and worked, worked and walked, me and Victory, fifteen miles to Palestine. That's where I met Violet. We got married and set up on Harlon Ricks' place near Tyrell. He owned the worst land in the county. Violet and me worked his crops for two years. When the soil ran out, when rocks was the biggest harvest, we ate what I shot. Then old man Ricks got fed up and sold the place along with our debt to a man called Clayton Bede. The debt rose from one hundred eighty dollars to eight hundred under him. Interest, he said, and all the fertilizer and stuff we got from the general store—things he paid for—the prices, he said, went up. Violet had to tend our place and walk the plow on his too, while I went from Bear to Crossland to Goshen working. Slash pine some of the time, sawmill most of it. Took us five years, but we did it.

"Then I got a job laying rail for the Southern Sky. I was twenty-eight years old and used to changing now, so in 1901, when Booker T. had a sandwich in the President's house, I was bold enough to do it again: decided to buy me a piece of land. Like a fool I thought they'd let me keep it. They ran us off with two slips of paper I never saw nor signed.

"I changed up again the fourth time in 1906 when I took my wife to Rome, a depot near where she was born, and boarded the Southern Sky for a northern one. They moved us five times in four different cars to abide by the Jim Crow law.

"We lived in a railroad flat in the Tenderloin. Violet went in service and I worked everything from whitefolks shoe leather to cigars in a room where they read to us while we rolled tobacco. I cleaned fish at night and toilets in the day till I got in with the table waiters. And I thought I had settled into my permanent self, the fifth one, when we left the stink of Mulberry Street and Little Africa, then the flesh-eating rats on West Fifty-third and moved uptown.

"By then all the hogs and cows had disappeared, and what used to be little shacky farms nowhere near the size of the piece I tried to buy was more and more houses. Used to be a colored man could get shot at just walking around up there. They built row houses and single ones with big yards and vegetable gardens. Then, just before the War, whole blocks was let to colored. Nice. Not like downtown. These had five, six rooms; some had ten and if you could manage fifty, sixty dollars a month, you could have one. When we moved from 140th Street to a bigger place on Lenox, it was the light-skinned renters who tried to keep us out. Me and Violet fought them, just like they was whites. We won. Bad times had hit then, and landlords white and black fought over colored people for the high rents that was okay by us because we got to live in five rooms even if some of us rented out two. The buildings were like castles in pictures and we who had cleaned up everybody's mess since the beginning knew better than anybody how to keep them nice. We had birds and plants everywhere, me and Violet. I gathered up the street droppings myself to fertilize them. And I made sure the front was as neat as the inside. I was doing hotel work by then. Better than waiting tables in a restaurant because in a hotel there're more ways to get tips. Pay was light, but the tips dropped in my palm fast as pecans in November.

"When the rents got raised and raised again, and the stores doubled the price of uptown beef and let the whitefolks' meat stay the same, I got me a little sideline selling Cleopatra products in the neighborhood. What with Violet cutting out day work and just doing hair, we did fine.

"Then long come a summer in 1917 and after those whitemen took that pipe from around my head, I was brand new for sure because they almost killed me. Along with many a more. One of those whitemen had a heart and kept the others from finishing me right then and there.

"I don't know exactly what started the riot. Could have been what the papers said, what the waiters I worked with said, or what Gistan said—that party, he said, where they sent out invitations to whites to come see a colored man burn alive. Gistan said thousands of whites turned up. Gistan said it sat on everybody's chest, and if the killing hadn't done it, something else would have. They were bringing in swarms of colored to work during the War. Crackers in the South mad cause Negroes were leaving; crackers in the North mad cause they were coming.

"I have seen some things in my time. In Virginia. Two of my stepbrothers. Hurt bad. Bad. Liked to kill Mrs. Rhoda. There was a girl, too. Visiting her folks up by Crossland. Just a girl. Anyway, up here if you bust out a hundred'll bust right along with you.

"I saw some little boys running in the street. One fell down and didn't get up right away, so I went over to him. That did it. Riot went on without me while me and Violet nursed my head. I survived it, though, and maybe that's what made me change again for the seventh time two years later in 1919 when I walked all the way, every goddamn step of the way, with the three six nine. Can't remember no time when I danced in the street but that one time when everybody did. I thought that change was the last, and it sure was the best because the War had come and gone and the colored troops of the three six nine that fought it made me so proud it split my heart in two. Gistan got me a job at another hotel where the tip was folding money more often than coin. I had it made. In 1925 we all had it made. Then Violet started sleeping with a doll in her arms. Too late. I understood in a way. In a way.

"Don't get me wrong. This wasn't Violet's fault. All of it's mine. All of it. I'll never get over what I did to that girl. Never. I changed once too often. Made myself new one time too many. You could say I've been a new Negro all my life. But all I lived through, all I seen, and not one of those changes prepared me for her. For Dorcas. You would have thought I was twenty, back in Palestine satisfying my appetite for the first time under a walnut tree.

"Surprised everybody when we left, me and Violet. They said the City makes you lonely, but since I'd been trained by the best woodsman ever, loneliness was a thing couldn't get near me. Shoot. Country boy; country man. How did I know what an eighteen-year-old girl might instigate in a grown man whose wife is sleeping with a doll? Make me know a loneliness I never could imagine in a forest empty of people for fifteen miles, or on a riverbank with nothing but live bait for company. Convince me I never knew the sweet side of anything until I tasted her honey. They say snakes go blind for a while before they shed skin for the last time.

. . .

"She had long hair and bad skin. A quart of water twice a day would have cleared it right up, her skin, but I didn't suggest it because I liked it like that. Little half moons clustered underneath her cheekbones, like faint hoofmarks. There and on her forehead. I bought the stuff she told me to, but glad none of it ever worked. Take my little hoof marks away? Leave me with no tracks at all? In this world the best thing, the only thing, is to find the trail and stick to it. I tracked my mother in Virginia and it led me right to her, and I tracked Dorcas from borough to borough. I didn't even have to work at it. Didn't even have to think. Something else takes over when the track begins to talk to you, give out its signs so strong you hardly have to look. If the track's not talking to you, you might get up out of your chair to go buy two or three cigarettes, have the nickel in your pocket and just start walking, then running, and end up somewhere in Staten Island, for crying out loud, Long Island, maybe, staring at goats. But if the trail speaks, no matter what's in the way, you can find yourself in a crowded room aiming a bullet at her heart, never mind it's the heart you can't live without.

"I wanted to stay there. Right after the gun went thuh! and nobody in there heard it but me and that is why the crowd didn't scatter like the flock of redwings they looked like but stayed pressed in, locked together by the steam of their dancing and the music, which would not let them go. I wanted to stay right there. Catch her before she fell and hurt herself.

"I wasn't looking for the trail. It was looking for me and when it started talking at first I couldn't hear it. I was rambling, just rambling all through the City. I had the gun but it was not the gun—it was my hand I wanted to touch you with. Five days rambling. First High Fashion on 131st Street because I thought you had a hair appointment on Tuesday. First Tuesday of every month it was. But you wasn't there. Some women came in with fish dinners from Salem Baptist, and the blind twins were playing guitar in the shop, and it's just like you said—only one of them's blind; the other one is just going along with the program. Probably not even brothers, let alone twins. Something their mama cooked up for a little extra change. They were playing something sooty, though; not the gospel like they usually do, and the women selling fish dinners frowned and talked about their mother bad, but they never said a word to the twins and I knew they were having a good time listening because one of the loudest ones could hardly suck her teeth for patting her foot. They didn't pay me no mind. Took me a while to get them to tell me you wasn't on the book for that day. Minnie said you had a touch-up Saturday and how she didn't approve of touch-ups not just because they were fifty cents instead of a dollar and a quarter for the whole do, but because it hurt the hair, heat on dirt she said, hurt the hair worse than anything she knew of. Except, of course, no heat at all. What did you have the touch-up for? That's what I first thought about. Last Saturday? You told me you were going with the choir out to Brooklyn to sing at Shiloh, and you had to leave at nine in the morning and wouldn't be back till night and that's why. And that you'd missed the last trip, and your aunt found out about it so you had to go on this one, and that's why. So I didn't wait for Violet to leave and unlock Malvonne's apartment. No need. But how could you have a touch-up the Saturday before and still make it to the station by nine o'clock in the morning when Minnie never opens up before noon on

Saturday because she's open till midnight getting everybody readied up for Sunday? And you didn't need to keep the Tuesday regular appointment, did you? I dismissed the evil in my thoughts because I wasn't sure that the sooty music the blind twins were playing wasn't the cause. It can do that to you, a certain kind of guitar playing. Not like the clarinets, but close. If that song had been coming through a clarinet, I'd have known right away. But the guitars—they confused me, made me doubt myself, and I lost the trail. Went home and didn't pick it up again until the next day when Malvonne looked at me and covered her mouth with her hand. Couldn't cover her eyes, though; the laugh came flying out of there.

"I know you didn't mean those things you said to me. After I found you and got you to come back to our room one more time. What you said I know you didn't mean. It hurt, though, and the next day I stood freezing on the stoop worrying myself sick about it. Nobody there but Malvonne sprinkling ashes on patches of ice. Across the street, leaning up against the iron railing, I saw three sweetbacks. Thirty degrees, not even ten in the morning, and they shone like patent leather. Smooth. Couldn't be more than twenty, twenty-two. Young. That's the City for you. One wore spats, and one had a handkerchief in his pocket same color as his tie. Had his coat draped across his shoulders. They were just leaning there, laughing and so on, and then they started crooning, leaning in, heads together, snapping fingers. City men, you know what I mean. Closed off to themselves, wise, young roosters. Didn't have to do a thing—just wait for the chicks to pass by and find them. Belted jackets and handkerchiefs the color of their ties. You think Malvonne would have covered her mouth in front of them? Or made roosters pay her in advance for the use of her place of a Thursday? Never would have happened because roosters don't need Malvonne. Chickens find the roosters and find the place, too, and if there is tracking to be done, they do it. They look; they figure. Roosters wait because they are the ones waited for. They don't have to trail anybody, look ignorant in a beauty parlor asking for a girl in front of women who couldn't wait for me to leave so they could pat on to the sooty music and talk about what the hell did I want to know about a girl not out of high school yet and wasn't I married to old crazy Violet? Only old cocks like me have to get up from the stoop, cut Malvonne off in the middle of a sentence and try to walk not run all the way to Inwood, where we sat the first time and you crossed your legs at the knees so I could see the green shoes you carried out the house in a paper sack so your aunt wouldn't know you tapped down Lenox and up Eighth in them instead of the oxfords you left the house in. While you flicked your foot, turned your ankles for the admiration of the heels, I looked at your knees but I didn't touch. I told you again that you were the reason Adam ate the apple and its core. That when he left Eden, he left a rich man. Not only did he have Eve, but he had the taste of the first apple in the world in his mouth for the rest of his life. The very first to know what it was like. To bite it, bite it down. Hear the crunch and let the red peeling break his heart.

"You looked at me then like you knew me, and I thought it really was Eden, and I couldn't take your eyes in because I was loving the hoof marks on your cheeks.

"I went back up there, to the very spot. Old snow made the sky soft and blackened tree bark. Dog tracks and rabbit too, neat as the pattern on a Sunday tie scattered over the snow. One of those dogs must have weighed eighty pounds. The rest were small size; one limped. My footprints messed everything up. And when I looked back at where I'd walked, saw myself standing there in street shoes, no galoshes, wet to the ankles, I knew. I didn't feel the cold, though, because I was remembering it the way it was in our time. That warm October, remember? The rose of Sharon was still heavy with flowers. Lilac trees, pines. That tulip tree where Indians gathered looked like a king. The first time we met there I got there before you. Two whitemen were sitting on a rock. I sat on the ground right next to them until they got disgusted and moved off. You had to be working or look like you was to be anywhere near there. That's why I brought my sample case along. To look like I was delivering something important. Yeah, it was forbidden, all right, but nobody loudtalked us that time. And it gave the thing an edge, being there, a danger that was more than me and you being together. I scratched our initials on the rock those men moved away from. D. and J. Later on, after we had a place and a routine, I brought you treats, worrying each time what to bring that would make you smile and come again the next time. How many phonograph records? How many silk stockings? The little kit to mend the runs, remember? The purple metal box with flowers on top full of Schrafft's chocolates. Cologne in a blue bottle that smelt like a whore. Flowers once, but you were disappointed with that treat, so I gave you a dollar to buy whatever you wanted with it. A whole day's pay back home when I was young. Just for you. Anything just for you. To bite down hard, chew up the core and have the taste of red apple skin to carry around for the rest of my life. In Malvonne's nephew's room with the iceman's sign in the window. Your first time. And mine, in a manner of speaking. For which, and I will say it again, I would strut out the Garden, strut! as long as you held on to my hand, girl. Dorcas, girl, your first time and mine. I *chose* you. Nobody gave you to me. Nobody said that's the one for you. I picked you out. Wrong time, yep, and doing wrong by my wife. But the picking out, the choosing. Don't ever think I fell for you, or fell over you. I didn't fall in love, I rose in it. I saw you and made up my mind. My mind. And I made up my mind to follow you too. That's something I know how to do from way back. Maybe I didn't tell you that part about me. My gift in the woods that even he looked up to and he was the best there ever was. Ever. Those old people, they knew it all. I talk about being new seven times before I met you, but back then, back there, if you was or claimed to be colored, you had to be new and stay the same every day the sun rose and every night it dropped. And let me tell you, baby, in those days it was more than a state of mind."

Risky, I'd say, trying to figure out anybody's state of mind. But worth the trouble if you're like me—curious, inventive and well-informed. Joe acts like he knew all about what the old folks did to keep on going, but he couldn't have known much about True Belle, for example, because I doubt Violet ever talked to him about her grandmother—and never about her mother. So he didn't know. Neither do I, although it's not hard to imagine what it must have been like.

Her state of mind when she moved from Baltimore back to Vesper County must have been a study. She'd left Wordsworth, the county seat, a slave, and returned in 1888 a free woman. Her daughter and grandchildren lived in a mean little place called Rome, twelve miles north of the town she'd left. The grandchildren ranged in age from four to fourteen, and one of them, Violet, was twelve years old when True Belle arrived. That was after the men had come for the stock, the pots and the chair her daughter Rose Dear was sitting in. When she got there all that was left, aside from some borrowed pallets and the clothes on their backs, was the paper Rose's husband had signed saying they could—that the men had the right to do it and, I suppose, the duty to do it, if the rain refused to rain, or if stones of ice fell from the sky instead and cut the crop down to its stalks. Nothing on the paper about the husband joining a party that favored niggers voting. Dispossessed of house and land, the sad little family True Belle found were living secretly in an abandoned shack some neighbors had located for them and eating what food these neighbors were able to share and the girls forage. Lots of okra and dried beans, and, since it was September, berries of every kind. Twice, however, the minister's son had brought them a young squirrel to feast on. Rose told people that her husband, fed up and stunned by the uselessness of his back and hands, tired of fried green tomatoes and grits, hungry beyond belief for the meat of some meat and not just its skin, furious at the price of coffee and the shape of his oldest girl's legs, had just quit. Got up and quit. Gone off somewhere to sit and think about it or sit and not think about it. It was better to make up talk than to let out what she knew. They might come looking for her next time, and not just her pots, her pans, her house. Lucky for her, True Belle was dying and willing to die in Vesper County, after giving her whole well life to Miss Vera Louise in Baltimore.

The death True Belle was dying took eleven years, long

enough for her to rescue Rose, bury her, see the husband return four times, make six quilts, thirteen shifts and fill Violet's head with stories about her whitelady and the light of both their lives—a beautiful young man whose name, for obvious reasons, was Golden Gray. Gray because that was Vera Louise's last name (much, much later it was also the color of his eyes), and Golden because after the pink birth-skin disappeared along with the down on his head, his flesh was radiantly golden, and floppy yellow curls covered his head and the lobes of his ears. It was nowhere as blond as Vera Louise's hair once was, but its sunlight color, its determined curliness, endeared him to her. Not all at once. It took a while. But True Belle laughed out loud the minute she laid eyes on him and thereafter every day for eighteen years.

When the three of them lived in a fine sandstone house on Edison Street in Baltimore, far away from Vesper County where both Vera Louise Gray and True Belle were born, what the whitelady told her neighbors and friends was partly true: that she could not bear the narrow little ways of her home county. And that she had brought her servant and an orphaned baby she fancied to Baltimore to experience a more sophisticated way of living.

It was a renegade, almost suffragette thing to do, and the neighbors and would-be women friends surrounded Vera Louise with as polite a distance as they could manage. If they thought that would force her to alter her manner, admit she needed to look for a husband—they were wrong. The out-of-state newcomer, rich and headstrong, contented herself with luxury and even less of their company. Besides she seemed taken up completely with book reading, pamphlet writing and the adoration of the orphan.

From the beginning, he was like a lamp in that quiet, shaded house. Simply startled each morning by the look of him, they vied with each other for the light he shed on them. He was given a fussy spoiling by Vera Louise and complete indulgence by True Belle, who, laughing, laughing, fed him test cakes and picked every single seed from the melon before she let him eat it. Vera Louise dressed him like the Prince of Wales and read him vivid stories.

True Belle, of course, would have known everything right away because, first of all, nobody could hide much in Wordsworth and nothing at all could be hidden in the Big Houses of its landowners. Certainly nobody could help noticing how many times a week a Negro boy from out Vienna way was called on to ride along with Miss Vera, and what part of the woods she preferred to ride in. True Belle knew what all the slaves knew, and she knew more since she was the one whose sole job it was to tend to whatever Miss Vera Louise wanted or needed, including doing her laundry, some of which had to be soaked overnight in vinegar once a month. So if it did not need it, if the personal garments could be washed along with the rest, True Belle knew why, and Vera Louise knew she knew. There was never any need to speak of it. The only people who didn't know were the fathers. The about-to-be father—the black boy—never found out, as far as True Belle could tell, because Vera Louise never mentioned his name or came near him ever again. The old father, Colonel Wordsworth Gray, didn't know a thing. Not one thing.

It had to be his wife who finally did tell him. Finally. Although she never spoke about it to her daughter, or, after she found out, ever spoke to her daughter at all, she was the one who would have had to let the Colonel know, and when he found out he stood up then sat down and then stood up again.

His left hand patted around the air searching for something: a shot of whiskey, his pipe, a whip, a shotgun, the Democratic platform, his heart—Vera Louise never knew. He looked hurt, deeply, deeply hurt for a few seconds. Then his rage seeped into the room, clouding the crystal and softening the starched tablecloth. Realizing the terrible thing that had happened to his daughter made him sweat, for there were seven mulatto children on his land. Sweat poured from his temples and collected under his chin; soaked his armpits and the back of his shirt as his rage swamped and flooded the room. The ivy on the table had perked up and the silver was slippery to the hand by the time he mopped his brow and gathered himself together to do an appropriate thing: slap Vera Louise into the serving table.

Her mother, however, had the final cut: her eyebrows were perfectly still but the look she gave Vera Louise as the girl struggled up from the floor was so full of repulsion the daughter could taste the sour saliva gathering under her mother's tongue, filling the insides of her cheeks. Only breeding, careful breeding, did not allow her to spit. No word, then or ever, passed between them. And the lingerie case full of money that lay on Vera's pillow the following Wednesday was, in its generosity, heavy with contempt. More money than anybody in the world needed for seven months or so away from home. So much money the message was indisputable: die, or live if you like, elsewhere.

True Belle was the one she wanted and the one she took. I don't know how hard it was for a slave woman to leave a husband that work and distance kept her from seeing much of anyhow, and to leave two daughters behind with an old aunt to take care of them. Rose Dear and May were eight and ten years old then. Good help at that age for anybody who owned them and no help at all to a mother who lived in Wordsworth, miles away from her husband in a rich man's house taking care of his daughter day and night. Perhaps it wasn't so hard to ask an older sister to look out for a husband and the girls because she was bound for Baltimore with Miss Vera Louise for a while. True Belle was twenty-seven and when would she ever get to see a great big city otherwise?

More important Miss Vera Louise might help her buy them all out with paper money, because she sure had a lot of it handed to her. Then again, maybe not. Maybe she frowned as she sat in the baggage car, rocking along with the boxes and trunks, unable to see the land she was traveling through. Maybe she felt bad. Anyway, choiceless, she went, leaving husband, sister, Rose Dear and May behind, and if she worried, the blond baby helped soothe her, and kept her entertained for eighteen years, until he left home.

So in 1888, with twenty-two years of the wages Miss Vera initiated soon as the War was over (but held in trust lest her servant get ideas), True Belle convinced herself and her mistress she was dying, got the money—ten eagle dollars—and was able to answer Rose Dear's pleas by coming back to Vesper with Baltimore tales for grandchildren she had never seen. She rented a small house, bought a cookstove for it and delighted the girls with descriptions of life with the wonderful Golden Gray. How they bathed him three times a day, and how the G on his underwear was embroidered with blue thread. The shape of the tub and what they put in the water to make him smell like honeysuckle sometimes and sometimes of lavender. How clever he was and how perfect a gentleman. The hilarious grown-up comments he made when a child and the cavalierlike courage he showed when he was a young man and went to find, then kill, if he was lucky, his father.

True Belle never saw him again after he rode off and didn't know if Vera Louise had any better luck. Her memories of the boy were more than enough.

I've thought about him a lot, wondered whether he was what True Belle loved and Violet too. Or the vain and hincty pinch-nose worrying about his coat and the ivory buttons on his waistcoat? Come all that way to insult not his father but his race.

Pretty hair can't be too long, Vera Louise once told him, and because she seemed to know such things, he believed her. Almost every other thing she said was false, but that last bit of information he held to be graven truth. So the yellow curls covered his coat collar like a farmer's, although the rightness of its length in fastidious Baltimore came from the woman who lied to him about practically everything including the question of whether she was his owner, his mother or a kindly neighbor. The other thing she did not lie about (although it took her eighteen years to get around to it) was that his father was a black-skinned nigger.

I see him in a two-seat phaeton. His horse is a fine one—black. Strapped to the back of the carriage is his trunk: large and crammed with beautiful shirts, linen, and embroidered sheets and pillow slips; a cigar case and silver toilet articles. A long coat, vanilla colored with dark brown cuffs and collar, is folded neatly beside him. He is a long way from home and it begins to rain furiously, but since it is August, he is not cold.

The left wheel strikes a stone and he hears, or thinks he does, a bump that may be the dislocation of his trunk. He reins in the horse and climbs down to see if any damage has been done to his things. He discovers that the trunk is loose—the rope has slipped and it is leaning. He unties everything and secures the rope more strongly.

Satisfied with his efforts, but annoyed at the heavy rain, the spoiling it is doing to his clothes and the speed of his journey, he looks around him. In the trees to his left, he sees a naked berry-black woman. She is covered with mud and leaves are in her hair. Her eyes are large and terrible. As soon as she sees him, she starts then turns suddenly to run, but in turning before she looks away she knocks her head against the tree she has been leaning against. Her terror is so great her body flees before her eyes are ready to find the route of escape. The blow knocks her out and down.

He looks at her and, holding on to the brim of his hat, moves quickly to get back into the carriage. He wants nothing to do with what he has seen—in fact he is certain that what he is running from is not a real woman but a "vision." When he picks up the reins he cannot help noticing that his horse is also black, naked and shiny wet, and his feelings about the horse are of security and affection. It occurs to him that there is something odd about that: the pride he takes in his horse; the nausea the woman provoked. He is a touch ashamed and decides to make sure it was a vision, that there is no naked black woman lying in the weeds.

He ties his horse to a sapling and sloshes back in driving rain to the place where the woman fell. She is still sprawled there. Her mouth and legs open. A small hickey is forming on her head. Her stomach is big and tight. He leans down, holding his breath against infection or odor or something. Something that might touch or penetrate him. She looks dead or deeply unconscious. And she is young. There is nothing he can do for her and for that he is relieved. Then he notices a rippling movement in her stomach. Something inside her is moving.

He does not see himself touching her, but the picture he does imagine is himself walking away from her a second time, climbing into his carriage and leaving her a second time. He is uneasy with this picture of himself, and does not want to spend any part of the time to come remembering having done that. Also there is something about where he has come from and why, where he is going and why that encourages in him an insistent, deliberate recklessness. The scene becomes an anecdote, an action that would unnerve Vera Louise and defend him against patricide. Maybe.

He unfolds his long coat that has been tucked in the seat beside him and throws it over the woman. Then he gathers her up in his arms and carries her, stumbling, since she is heavier than he supposed, to the carriage. With great difficulty, he gets her into a sitting position in the carriage. Her head is leaning away from him and her feet are touching one of his splendid but muddy boots. He is hoping her lean will not shift, although there is nothing he can do about the dirty bare feet against his boot, for if he shifts her again, she may swerve over to his and not her side of the carriage. As he urges the horse on, he is gentle for fear the ruts and the muddy road will cause her to fall forward or brush him in some way.

He is heading toward a house a little ways out from a town named Vienna. It is the house where his father lives. And now he thinks it is an interesting, even comic idea to meet this nigger whom he has never seen (and who has never tried to see him) with an armful of black, liquid female. Provided, of course, she does not wake and the rippling in her stomach remains light. That bothers him—that she might regain consciousness and become something more than his own dark purpose.

He has not looked at her for some time. Now he does and notices a trickle of blood down her jaw onto her neck. The hickey that rose when she smashed into the tree is not the cause of her faint; she must have struck her head on a rock or something when she fell. But she is breathing still. Now he hopes she will not die—not yet, not until he gets to the house described and mapped out for him in clear, childish pictures by True Belle.

The rain seems to be following him; whenever he thinks it is about to stop, a few yards on it gets worse. He has been traveling for six hours, at least, and has been assured by the innkeeper that the journey would end before dark. Now he is not so sure. He doesn't relish night coming on with that passenger. He is calmed by the valley opening before him—the one it should take an hour to get through before he reaches the house a mile or two this side of Vienna. Quite suddenly, the rain stops. It is the longest hour, filled with recollections of luxury and pain. When he gets to the house, he pulls into the yard and finds a shed with two stalls in back. He takes his horse into one and wipes her down carefully. Then he throws a blanket over her and looks about for water and feed. He takes a long time over this. It is important to him, and he is not sure he is not being watched by someone in the house. In fact, he hopes he is; hopes the nigger is watching open-mouthed from a crack in the planks that serve as wall.

But no one comes out to speak to him, so perhaps there is no one. After the horse is seen to (and he has noticed that one shoe needs repair), he returns to the carriage for his trunk. He unlashes it and hoists it to his shoulder. It makes a further mess of his waistcoat and silk shirt as he carries it into the house. On the little porch, he makes no attempt to knock and the door is closed but not latched. He enters and looks about for a suitable place for his trunk. He sets it down on the dirt floor and examines the house. It has two rooms: a cot in each, table, chair, fireplace, cookstove in one. Modest, lived in, male, but otherwise no indication of the personality of its owner. The cookstove is cold, and the fireplace has a heap of ash, but no embers. The occupant has been gone perhaps a day, maybe two.

After he has seen to the placement of his trunk, he goes back to the carriage to get the woman. The removal of the trunk has displaced the weight, and the carriage is tipping a little on its axis. He reaches in the door and pulls her out. Her skin is almost too hot to handle. The long coat around her drags in the mud as he carries her into the house. He lays her down on a cot, and then curses himself for not having pulled its blanket back first. Now she is on top of it and the coat is all there seems to be to cover her. Its ruin may be permanent. He goes into the second room, and examining a wooden box there, finds a woman's dress. Gingerly he retrieves his coat and covers the woman with the strange-smelling dress. Now he opens his own trunk and selects a white cotton shirt and flannel waistcoat. He drapes the fresh shirt on the single chair rather than risk damaging it on a nail hammered in the wall. Carefully he examines the dry things. Then he sets about trying to make a fire. There is wood in the wood box and the fireplace, and in the darkest corner of the room a can of kerosene which he sprinkles on the wood. But no matches. For a long time he looks for matches and finally finds some in a can, wrapped in a bit of ticking. Five matches, to be exact. The kerosene has evaporated from the wood by the time he locates the matches. He is not adept at this. Other people have always lit the fires in his life. But he persists and at last has a good roaring flame. Now he can sit down, smoke a cigar and prepare himself for the return of the man who lives there. A man he assumes is named Henry LesTroy, although from the way True Belle pronounced it, it could be something else. A man of no consequence, except a tiny reputation as a tracker based on one or two escapades signaling his expertise in reading trails. A long time ago, according to True Belle, who gave him all the details—since Vera Louise shut herself in the bedroom or turned her head whenever he tried to pull information from her. Henry Lestory or LesTroy or something like that, but who cares what the nigger's name is. Except the woman who regretted ever knowing him at all and locked her door rather than say it out loud. And would have regretted the baby he gave her too, given it away, except it was golden and she had never seen that color except in the morning sky and in bottles of champagne. True Belle told him Vera Louise had smiled and said, "But he's golden. Completely golden!" So they named him that and didn't take him to the Catholic Foundling Hospital, where whitegirls deposited their mortification.

He has known all that for seven days, eight now. And he has known his father's name and the location of the house he once lived in for two. Information that came from the woman who cooked and cleaned for Vera Louise; who sent baskets of plum preserves, ham and loaves of bread every week while he was in boarding school; who gave his frayed shirts to rag-and-bone men rather than let him wear them; the woman who smiled and shook her head every time she looked at him. Even when he was a tiny boy with a head swollen with fat champagne-colored curls, and ate the pieces of cake she held out to him, her smile was more amusement than pleasure. When the two of them, the whitewoman and the cook, bathed him they sometimes passed anxious looks at the palms of his hand, the texture of his drying hair. Well, Vera Louise was anxious; True Belle just smiled, and now he knew what she was smiling about, the nigger. But so was he. He had always thought there was only one kind—True Belle's kind. Black and nothing. Like Henry LesTroy. Like the filthy woman snoring on the cot. But there was another kind—like himself.

The rain has stopped for good, apparently. He looks about for something to eat that doesn't need to be cooked—ready made. He has found nothing but a jug of liquor. He continues to sample it and sits back down before the fire.

In the silence left by the rain that has stopped, he hears hoofbeats. Beyond the door he sees a rider staring at his carriage. He approaches. Hello. Might you be related to Lestory? Henry LesTroy or whatever his name is?

The rider doesn't blink.

"No, sir. Vienna. Be back direcklin."

He doesn't understand any of it. And he is drunk now anyway. Happily. Perhaps he can sleep now. But he shouldn't. The owner of the house might return, or the liquid black woman might wake or die or give birth or . . .

When he stopped the buggy, got out to tie the horse and walk back through the rain, perhaps it was because the awful-looking thing lying in wet weeds was everything he was not as well as a proper protection against and anodyne to what he believed his father to be, and therefore (if it could just be contained, identified)—himself. Or was the figure, the vision as he thought of it, a thing that touched him before its fall?

The thing he saw in the averted glance of the servants at his boarding school; the bootblack who tap-danced for a penny. A vision that, at the moment when his scare was sharpest, looked also like home comfortable enough to wallow in? That could be it. But who could live in that leafy hair? that unfathomable skin? But he already had lived in and with it: True Belle had been his first and major love, which may be why two gallops beyond that hair, that skin, their absence was unthinkable. And if he shuddered at the possibility of her leaning on him, of her sliding a bit to the left and actually resting while she slept on his shoulder, it is also true that he overcame the shudder. Swallowed, maybe, and clicked the horse.

I like to think of him that way. Sitting straight in the carriage. Rain matting the hair over his collar, forming a little pool in the space between his boots. His gray-eyed squint as he tries to see through sheets of water. Then without warning as the road enters a valley the rain stops and there is a white grease pat of a sun cooking up there in its sky. Now he can hear things outside himself. Soaked leaves disentangling themselves one from another. The plop of nuts and the flutter of partridge removing their beaks from their hearts. Squirrels, having raced to limb tips, poise there to assess danger. The horse tosses her head to scatter a hovering cloud of gnats. So carefully is he listening he does not see the one-mile marker with VIENNA carved vertically in the stone. He passes it by and then sees the roof of a cabin not five furlongs ahead. It could belong to anyone, anyone at all. But maybe, along with the pity of its fence enclosing a dirt yard in which a rocker without arms lies on its side, the door fastened with a bit of rope for a lock but gaping at its hinges, maybe it shelters his father.

Golden Gray reins in his horse. This is a thing he does well.

The other is play the piano. Dismounting, he leads the horse close enough to look. Animals are somewhere; he can smell them, but the little house looks empty, if not cast-off completely. Certainly the owner never expected a horse and carriage to arrive—the fence gate is wide enough for a stout woman but no more. He unharnesses the horse and walks it a way to the right and discovers, behind the cabin and under a tree he does not know the name of, two open stalls, one of which is full of shapes. Leading the horse he hears behind him a groan from the woman, but doesn't stop to see whether she is waking or dying or falling off the seat. Close up on the stalls he sees that the shapes are tubs, sacks, lumber, wheels, a broken plow, a butter press and a metal trunk. There is a stake too, and he ties the horse to it. Water, he thinks. Water for the horse. What he thinks is a pump in the distance is an ax handle still lodged in a stump. There was the downpour though, and a good bit of it has collected in a washtub near the chopping stump. So his horse can be watered, but where are the other animals he smells but does not see or hear? Out of the shaft, the horse drinks greedily and the carriage tips dangerously with the unequal distribution of his trunk and the woman. Golden Gray examines the trunk fastenings before going to the rope-locked door of the little house.

That is what makes me worry about him. How he thinks first of his clothes, and not the woman. How he checks the fastenings, but not her breath. It's hard to get past that, but then he scrapes the mud from his Baltimore soles before he enters a cabin with a dirt floor and I don't hate him much anymore.

Inside, light comes slowly, and, tired after forcing its way through oiled paper tacked around a window set into the back wall, rests on the dirt floor unable to reach higher than Golden

Gray's waist. The grandest thing in the room is the fireplace. Clean, set for a new fire, braced with scoured stones, from which two metal arms for holding kettles extend. As for the rest: a cot, wooden, a rust-colored wool blanket fitted neatly over a thin and bumpy mattress. Not cobs, certainly not feathers or leaves. Rags. Bits of truly unusable fabric shoved into a ticking shroud. It reminds Golden Gray of the pillow True Belle made for King to sleep on at her feet. She had been given the name of a powerful male dog, but she was a cat without personality, which is why True Belle liked her and wanted her close by. Two beds and one chair, as it turns out. The person who lived here sat alone at the table, but had two beds: one in a second room entered by a door stronger and better-made than the one to the house itself. And in that room, the second one, is a box and a woman's green frock folded on top of its contents. He looks, just as casual as you please. Lifts up the lid and sees the dress and would dig deeper, but the dress reminds him of what should have been in the front of his mind: the woman breathing through her mouth in the other room. Does he think she will wake up and run off, relieving him of his choice, if he leaves her alone? Or that she will be dead, which is the same thing.

He is avoiding her, I know. Having done the big thing, the hard thing, by going back and lifting the girl up from weeds that clung to his trousers, by not looking to see what he could see of her private parts, the shock of knowing the hair there, once it was dry, was thick enough to part with a fingernail. He tried not to look at the hair on her head either, or at her face, turned away into blades of grass. Already he had seen the deer eyes that fixed on him through the rain, fixed on him as she backed away, fixed on him as her body began to turn for flight.

Too bad she didn't have the sense of a deer and hadn't looked in the direction she was going soon enough to see the giant maple in time. In time. When he went back for her he did not know if she was still there—she could have gotten up and run away—but he believed, hoped, the deer eyes would be closed. Suddenly he was not sure of himself. They might be open. His gratitude that they were not gave him the strength he needed to lift her.

After fidgeting with his trunk he steps into the yard. The sunlight bangs his own eyes shut and he holds his hand over them, peeking through his fingers until it is safe. The sigh he makes is deep, a hungry air-take for the strength and perseverance all life, but especially his, requires. Can you see the fields beyond, crackling and drying in the wind? The blade of blackbirds rising out of nowhere, brandishing and then gone? The odor of the invisible animals accentuated in the heat mixing now with out-of-control mint and something fruity needing to be picked. No one is looking at him, but he behaves as though there is. That's the way. Carry yourself the way you would if you were always under the reviewing gaze of an impressionable but casual acquaintance.

She is still there. Hardly distinguishable from the shadow of the carriage hood under which she sleeps. Everything about her is violent, or seems so, but that is because she is exposed under that long coat, and there is nothing to prevent Golden Gray from believing that an exposed woman will explode in his arms, or worse, that he will, in hers. She should be stuffed into the ticking along with the bits of rag, stitched shut to hide her visible lumps and moving parts. But she is there and he looks into the shadow to find her face, and her deer eyes, too, if he has to. The deer eyes are closed, and thank God will not open easily, for they are sealed with blood. A lip of skin hangs from her forehead and the blood from it has covered her eyes, her nose and one cheek before it jelled. Darker than the blood though are her lips, thick enough to laugh at and to break his heart.

I know he is a hypocrite; that he is shaping a story for himself to tell somebody, to tell his father, naturally. How he was driving along, saw and saved this wild black girl: No qualms. I had no qualms. See look, here, how it ruined my coat and soiled beyond repair a shirt you will never see another one of. I have gloves made from the hide of a very young cow, but I did not use them to hoist her, carry her. I touched her with my bare hands. From the weeds to the carriage; from the carriage into this cabin that could belong to anyone. Anyone at all. I laid her on the wooden cot first thing because she was heavier than she looked, and in my haste forgot to lift the blanket first to cover her. I thought of the blood, I think, dirtying the mattress. But who could tell if it was already dirty or not? I didn't want to lift her again, so I went into the other room and got the dress I found there and draped it best I could over her. She looked more naked then than before I covered her, but there was nothing else I could do.

He is lying, the hypocrite. He could have opened his big fat trunk; removed one of the two hand-embroidered sheets, or even his dressing gown, and covered the girl. He's young. So young. He thinks his story is wonderful, and that if spoken right will impress his father with his willingness, his honor. But I know better. He wants to brag about this encounter, like a knight errant bragging about his coolness as he unscrews the spike from the monster's heart and breathes life back into the fiery nostrils. Except this monster without scales or flaming breath is more dangerous for she is a bloody-faced girl of moving parts, of luminous eyes and lips to break your heart.

Why doesn't he wipe her face, I wonder. She is more savage perhaps this way. More graphically rescued. If she should rise up and claw him it would satisfy him even more and confirm True Belle's warning about the man who saved the rattler, nursed the rattler, fed the rattler only to discover that the last piece of information he would have on earth was the irrevocable nature of the rattler. Aw, but he is young, young and he is hurting, so I forgive him his self-deception and his grand, fake gestures, and when I watch him sipping too quickly the cane liquor he has found, worrying about his coat and not tending to the girl, I don't hate him at all. He has a pistol in his trunk and a silver cigar case, but he is a boy after all, and he sits at the table in the single chair contemplating changing into fresh clothes, for the ones he is wearing, still wet at the seams and cuffs, are filthy with sweat, blood and soil. Should he retrieve the broken rocker from the front yard? Go check on the horse? He is thinking about that, his next move, when he hears slow, muffled hoof clops. Glancing at the girl to make sure the dress and the blood are intact, he opens the door and peers into the yard. Floating toward him parallel to the fence is a black boy astride a mule.

He would have said, "Morning," although it wasn't, but he thought the man lurching down the steps was white and not to be spoken to without leave. Drunk, too, he thought, because his clothes were those of a gent who sleeps in his own yard after a big party rather than in his wife's bed, and wakes when his dogs come to lick his face. He thought this whiteman, this drunken gent, was looking for Mr. Henry, waiting for him, needing the wild turkeys now, now, goddamn it—or the pelts, or whatever it was Mr. Henry promised, owed or sold.

"Hello," said the drunken gent, and if the black boy doubted for a minute whether he was white, the smileless smile that came with the greeting convinced him.

"Sir."

"You live around here?"

"No, sir."

"No? Where from then?"

"Out Vienna way."

"Is that right? Where you on your way to?"

It was better when they asked questions most times. If they said anything flat out it was something nobody wanted to hear. The boy picked at the burlap of his sack. "See bout the stock. Mr. Henry he say I'm to see bout it."

See that? The smile was gone. "Henry?" the man asked. His face was another color now. More blood in it. "You said Henry?"

"Yes, sir."

"Where is he? Is he close?"

"Don't know, sir. Gone off."

"Where does he live. What house?"

Oh, thought the boy, he doesn't know Mr. Henry but he's looking for him. "This here one."

"What?"

"This here place his."

"This? This is his? He lives here?"

The blood left his face and showed up his eyes better. "Yes, sir. When he home. Ain't home now."

Golden Gray frowned. He thought he would know it right

away, without being told and, surprised that he had, he turned around to look at it. "You sure? You sure this is where he lives? Henry Lestroy?"

"Yes, sir."

"When's he coming back?"

"Any day now."

Golden Gray ran his thumb across his bottom lip. He lifted his eyes from the boy's face and stared out across the fields still cracking in the wind. "What did you say you come by here for?"

"See bout his stock."

"What stock? There's nothing here but my horse."

"Out back." He pointed with his eyes and a gesture of his hand. "They roam now and again. Mr. Henry he say I'm to look see they get back if they break out."

Golden Gray didn't hear the pride in the boy's voice: "Mr. Henry say *I'm* . . ." because he was so terrified he laughed.

This was it, then. The place he meant to come to and any day now the blackest man in the world would be there too. "All right, then. Go on about it then."

The boy tsched his mule—for nothing, apparently, because he had to kick his sides with creamy heels before the animal obeyed.

"Say!" Golden Gray held up his hand. "When you're done, come back here. I want you to help me with something. Hear?"

"Yes, sir. I be back."

Golden Gray went into the second room to change his clothes—this time he chose something formal, elegant. It was the right time to do it. To select a very fine shirt; to unfold the dark blue trousers that fit just so. The right time and the only time for as long as anyone in Vienna knew him he wore the clothes he put on at that moment. When he took them out and laid them carefully on the cot—the yellow shirt, the trousers with buttons of bone in the fly, the butter-colored waistcoat—the arrangement, lying on the bed, looked like an empty man with one arm folded under. He sat down on the rough mattress near the trouser cuffs, and when dark spots formed on the cloth he saw that he was crying.

Only now, he thought, now that I know I have a father, do I feel his absence: the place where he should have been and was not. Before, I thought everybody was one-armed, like me. Now I feel the surgery. The crunch of bone when it is sundered, the sliced flesh and the tubes of blood cut through, shocking the bloodrun and disturbing the nerves. They dangle and writhe. Singing pain. Waking me with the sound of itself, thrumming when I sleep so deeply it strangles my dreams away. There is nothing for it but to go away from where he is not to where he used to be and might be still. Let the dangle and the writhe see what it is missing; let the pain sing to the dirt where he stepped in the place where he used to be and might be still. I am not going to be healed, or to find the arm that was removed from me. I am going to freshen the pain, point it, so we both know what it is for.

And no, I am not angry. I don't need the arm. But I do need to know what it could have been like to have had it. It's a phantom I have to behold and be held by, in whatever crevices it lies, under whatever branch. Or maybe it stalks treeless and open places, lit with an oily sun. This part of me that does not know me, has never touched me or lingered at my side. This gone-away hand that never helped me over the stile, or guided me past the dragons, pulled me up from the ditch into which

I stumbled. Stroked my hair, fed me food; took the far end of the load to make it easier for me to carry. This arm that never held itself out, extended from my body, to give me balance as I walked thin rails or logs, round and slippery with danger. When I find it, will it wave to me? Gesture, beckon to me to come along? Or will it even know who or what I am? It doesn't matter. I will locate it so the severed part can remember the snatch, the slice of its disfigurement. Perhaps then the arm will no longer be a phantom, but will take its own shape, grow its own muscle and bone, and its blood will pump from the loud singing that has found the purpose of its serenade. Amen.

Who will take my part? Soap away the shame? Suds it till it falls away muck at my feet to be stepped out of? Will he? Redeem me like a pawn ticket worth little on the marketplace, but priceless in retrieving real value? What do I care what the color of his skin is, or his contact with my mother? When I see him, or what is left of him, I will tell him all about the missing part of me and listen for his crying shame. I will exchange then; let him have mine and take his as my own and we will both be free, arm-tangled and whole.

It had rocked him when he heard who and what his father was. Made him loose, lost. He had first fingered then torn some of his mother's clothes and sat in the grass looking at the things scattered on the lawn as well as in his mind. Little lights moving like worms frolicked before his eyes, and the breath of despair had a nasty smell. It was True Belle who helped him up from the grass, soaped his tangled hair and told him what he had to do.

"Go on," she said. "I'll tell you how to find him, or what's left of him. It don't matter if you do find him or not; it's the going that counts."

So he collected what she said he should collect, packed it all and set out. During the journey he worried a lot about what he looked like, what armor he could call on. There was nothing but his trunk and the set of his jaw. But he was ready, ready to meet the black and savage man who bothered him and abused his arm.

Instead he met, ran into, a wild black girl smashing herself in the head with fright, who lay now in the other room while a black boy was rounding up stock outside. He thought she would be his lance and shield; now he would have to be his own. Look into the deer eyes with the dawning gray of his own. He needs courage for that, but he has it. He has the courage to do what Duchesses of Marlborough do all the time: relinquish being an adored bud clasping its future, and dare to open wide, to let the layers of its petals go flat, show the cluster of stamens dead center for all to see.

What was I thinking of? How could I have imagined him so poorly? Not noticed the hurt that was not linked to the color of his skin, or the blood that beat beneath it. But to some other thing that longed for authenticity, for a right to be in this place, effortlessly without needing to acquire a false face, a laughless grin, a talking posture. I have been careless and stupid and it infuriates me to discover (again) how unreliable I am. Even his horse had understood and borne Golden Gray along with just a touch or two of the whip. Steadily it had plodded, through valleys without trails, through streams without bridges or ferries for crossing. Eye gaze just above the road, undistracted by the small life that darted toward its hooves, heaving its great chest forward, pacing to hold on to its strength and gather more. It did not know where it was going and it knew nothing of the way, but it did know the nature of its work. Get there, said its hooves. If we can just get there.

Now I have to think this through, carefully, even though I may be doomed to another misunderstanding. I have to do it and not break down. Not hating him is not enough; liking, loving him is not useful. I have to alter things. I have to be a shadow who wishes him well, like the smiles of the dead left over from their lives. I want to dream a nice dream for him, and another of him. Lie down next to him, a wrinkle in the sheet, and contemplate his pain and by doing so ease it, diminish it. I want to be the language that wishes him well, speaks his name, wakes him when his eyes need to be open. I want him to stand next to a well dug quite clear from trees so twigs and leaves will not fall into the deep water, and while standing there in shapely light, his fingertips on the rim of stone, his gaze at no one thing, his mind soaked and sodden with sorrow, or dry and brittle with the hopelessness that comes from knowing too little and feeling too much (so brittle, so dry he is in danger of the reverse: feeling nothing and knowing everything). There then, with nothing available but the soaking or the brittleness, not even looking toward the well, not aware of its mossy, unpleasant odor, or the little life that hovers at its rim, but to stand there next to it and from down in it, where the light does not reach, a collection of leftover smiles stirs, some brief benevolent love rises from the darkness and there is nothing for him to see or hear, and there is no reason to stay but he does. For the safety at first, then for the company. Then for himself—with a kind of confident, enabling, serene power that flicks like a razor and then hides. But he has felt it now, and it may come again. No doubt a lot of other things will come again: doubt will come, and things may seem unclear from time to time. But once the razor blade has flicked—he will remember it, and if he remembers it he can recall it. That is to say, he has it at his disposal.

. . .

The boy was thirteen and had seen enough people slumped over a plow, or stilled after childbirth, and enough drowned children to know the difference between the quick and the dead. What he saw lying on the cot under a shiny green dress he believed was alive. The boy never raised his eyes from the girl's face (except when Golden Gray said, "I found that dress in there and covered her with it"). He glanced toward the second room and back at the man he believed was white. The boy lifted the sleeve of the dress and patted the slash on the girl's forehead. Her face was fire hot. The blood was dry as skin.

"Water," he said and left the cabin.

Golden Gray started to follow him but stood in the doorway unable to go forward or back. The boy returned with a bucket of well water and an empty burlap sack. He dipped a cup into the water, dribbled some into her mouth. She neither swallowed nor stirred.

"How long she been out?"

"Less than an hour," said Golden Gray.

The boy knelt down to clean her face, slowly lifting whole patches of blood from her cheek, her nose, one eye, then the other. Golden Gray watched and he thought he was ready for those deer eyes to open.

A thing like that could harm you. Thirteen years after Golden Gray stiffened himself to look at that girl, the harm she could do was still alive. Pregnant girls were the most susceptible, but so were the grandfathers. Any fascination could mark a newborn: melons, rabbits, wisteria, rope, and, more than a shed snakeskin, a wild woman is the worst of all. So the warnings the girls got were part of a whole group of things to look out for lest the baby come here craving or favoring the mother's distraction. Who would have thought old men needed to be cautioned too; told and warned against seeing, smelling or even hearing her?

She lived close, they said, not way off in the woods or even down in the riverbed, but somewhere in that cane field—at its edge some said or maybe moving around in it. Close. Cutting cane could get frenzied sometimes when young men got the feeling she was just yonder, hiding, and probably looking at them. One swing of the cutting blade could lop off her head if she got sassy or too close, and it would be her own fault. That would be when they cut bad—when the cane stalks flew up to slam the face, or the bill would slip and cut a coworker nearby. Just thinking about her, whether she was close or not, could mess up a whole morning's work.

The grandfathers, way past slashing but still able enough to bind stalks or feed the sugar vats, used to be thought safe. That is until the man the grandfathers called Hunters Hunter got tapped on the shoulder by fingertips that couldn't be anybody's but hers. When the man snapped up, he saw the cane stalks shuddering but he didn't hear a single crack. Because he was more used to wood life than tame, he knew when the eyes watching him were up in a tree, behind a knoll or, like this, at ground level. You can see how he was confused: the fingertips at his shoulder, the eyes at his feet. First thing came to mind was the woman he named himself some thirteen years ago because, while tending her, that was the word he thought of: Wild. He was sure he was tending a sweet but abused young girl at first, but when she bit him, he said, Oh, she's wild. Thinking, some things are like that. There's no gain fathoming more.

He remembered her laugh, though, and how peaceful she was the first few days following the bite, so the touch of her fingertips didn't frighten him, but it did make him sad. Too sad to report the sighting to his coworkers, old men like himself no longer able to cut all day. Unwarned, they weren't prepared for the way their blood felt when they caught a glimpse of her, or for how trembly their legs got hearing that babygirl laugh. The pregnant girls marked their babies or didn't, but the grandfathers—unwarned—went soft in the head, walked out of the syrup house, left their beds in the shank of the night, wet themselves, forgot the names of their grown children and where they'd put their razor strops.

When the man they called Hunters Hunter knew her—tended her—she was touchy. If he had handled it right, maybe she would have stayed in the house, nursed her baby, learned how to dress and talk to folks. Every now and then when he thought about her he was convinced she was dead. When for months there was no sign or sound of her, he sighed and relived that time when his house was full of motherlessness—and the chief unmothering was Wild's. Local people used the story of her to caution children and pregnant girls and it saddened him to learn that instead of resting she was hungry still. Though for what, exactly, he couldn't say, unless it was for hair the color of a young man's name. To see the two of them together was a regular jolt: the young man's head of yellow hair long as a dog's tail next to her skein of black wool.

He didn't report it, but the news got out anyway: Wild was not a story of a used-to-be-long-ago-crazy girl whose neck cane cutters liked to imagine under the blade, or a quick and early stop for hardheaded children. She was still out there—and real. Someone saw the man they called Hunters Hunter jump, grab his shoulder and, when he turned around to gaze at the cane field, murmur loud enough for somebody to hear, "Wild. Dog me, if it ain't Wild." The pregnant girls just sighed at the news and went on sweeping and sprinkling the dirt yards, and the young men sharpened their blades till the edges whistled. But the old men started dreaming. They remembered when she came, what she looked like, why she stayed and that queer boy she set so much store by.

Not too many people saw the boy. The first wasn't Hunters Hunter, who was off looking for enough fox to sell. The first was Patty's boy, Honor. He was looking in on Mr. Henry's place while he was gone, and on one of the days he stopped by—to do a little weeding maybe and see if the pigs and chickens were still alive—it rained all morning. Sheets of it made afternoon rainbows everywhere. Later he told his mother that the whole cabin was rainbowed and when the man came out the door, and Honor looked at his wet yellow hair and creamy skin, he thought a ghost had taken over the place. Then he realized he was looking at a whiteman and never believed otherwise, even though he saw Mr. Henry's face when the whiteman told him he was his son.

When Henry Lestory, the man so expert in the woods he'd become a hunter's hunter (and when spoken of and to, that is what they called him), got back and saw the buggy and the beautiful horse tied near his stall, he was instantly alarmed. No man he knew drove a carriage like that; no horse in the county had its mane cut and combed that way. Then he saw the mule Patty's boy rode and calmed down a bit. He stood in his own door and had a hard time making out what he was looking at. Patty's boy, Honor, was kneeling beside the cot on which a pregnant girl lay, and a golden-haired man towered above them both. There had never been a whiteman inside his house. Hunters Hunter swallowed. All the pains he had taken shot to hell.

When the blond man turned to look at him, the gray eyes

widened, then closed, then, sliding slowly up from Hunter's boots to his knees, to chest to head, the man's gaze was like a tongue. By the time the gray eyes were level with his, Hunter had to struggle to keep from feeling trapped—in his own house. Even the groan from the cot did not break the lock of the stranger's stare. Everything about him was young and soft—except the color of his eyes.

Honor looked from one to the other. "Glad you back, Mr. Henry."

"Who be these?"

"They both in here before me."

"Who *be* these?"

"Can't say, sir. The woman she bad but coming around now."

The golden-haired man had no pistol Hunter could see, and his thin boots had never walked country roads. His clothes would make a preacher sigh and Hunter knew from the ladylike hands the stranger had never made a fist hard enough to smash a melon. He walked to the table and placed his pouch on it. With one swing he tossed a brace of woodcock in the corner. But he kept his rifle in the crook of his arm. And his hat on his head. The gray eyes followed his every move.

"The woman had a bad fall from what I can tell. This here gent, he carried her in here. I cleaned the blood up best I could."

Hunter noticed the green dress covering the woman, the black-blood spots on the sleeve.

"I got the fowl in and most of the pigs. Cept Bubba. He young but getting big, Mr. Henry. Big and mean . . ."

The cane-liquor bottle, uncapped, was on the table, a tin cup next to it. Hunter checked its contents and eased the stopper in, wondering what land this queer man came from who knew so little about the rules of hospitality. Woodsmen, white or black, all country people were free to enter a lean-to, a hunter's shooting cabin. Take what they needed, leave what they could. They were waystations and anybody, everybody, might have need of shelter. But nobody, nobody, drank a man's liquor in his house unless they knew each other mighty well.

"Do we know one another?" Hunter thought the "sir" he left out was as loud as a bang. But the man didn't hear it because he had a bang of his own.

"No. Daddy. We don't."

He couldn't say it wasn't possible. That he needed a midwife or a locket portrait to convince him. But the shock was heavy just the same.

"I never knew you were in the world" was what he said eventually, but what the blond man had to say, planned to say in response, had to wait because the woman screamed then and hoisted herself on her elbows to look between her raised knees.

The city man looked faint, but Honor and Hunter had not only watched the common and counted-on birthings farm people see, but had tugged and twisted newborns from all sorts of canals. This baby was not easy. It clung to the walls of that foamy cave, and the mother was of practically no help. When the baby finally emerged, the problem was clear immediately: the woman would not hold the baby or look at it. Hunter sent the boy home.

"Tell your maw to get one of the women to come out here. Come out here and take it. Otherwise it won't live out the morrow."

"Yes sir!"

"And bring cane liquor if any's around."

"Yes sir!"

Hunter bent down then to look at the mother, who hadn't said anything since that scream. Sweat covered her face and, breathing hard, she licked beads of it off her upper lip. He leaned closer. Under the dirt, lacing her coal-black skin, were traces of bad things; like tobacco juice, brine and a craftsman's sense of play. When he turned his head to adjust the blanket over her, she raised up and sank her teeth in his cheek. He yanked away and touching his bruised face lightly, chuckled. "Wild, eh?" He turned to look at the pale boy-man who had called him "Daddy."

"Where you pick up a wild woman?"

"In the woods. Where wild women grow."

"Say who she was?"

The man shook his head. "I startled her. She hit her head on a rock slab. I couldn't just leave her there."

"Reckon not. Who sent you to me?"

"True Belle."

"Ahhhh." Hunter smiled. "Where is she? I never did hear where she went off to."

"Or with?"

"Went off with the Colonel's daughter. Colonel Wordsworth Gray. Everybody knowed that. Quick they went, too."

"Guess why."

"Don't have to guess now. I never knew you was in the world."

"Did you think about her? Wonder where she was?"

"True Belle?"

"No! Vera. Vera Louise."

"Aw, man. What I look like wondering where a whitegirl went?"

"My mother!"

"Suppose I did, eh? What'd be the next step? Go up to the Colonel? Say, look here, Colonel Gray, I been wondering where your daughter got to. We ain't been riding in a while. Tell you what you do. Tell her I'm waiting for her and to come on out. She'll know the place we meet at. And tell her to wear that green dress. The one make it hard to see her in the grass." Hunter passed his hand over his jaw. "You ain't said where they at. Where you come from."

"Baltimore. My name is Golden Gray."

"Can't say it don't suit."

"Suit you if it was Golden Lestory?"

"Not in these parts." Hunter slipped his hand under the baby's blanket to see if its heart was going. "Baby boy's weak. Got to get some nursing soon."

"How touching."

"Look here. What you want? I mean, now; what you want now? Want to stay here? You welcome. Want to chastise me? Throw it out your mind. I won't take a contrary word. You come in here, drink my liquor, rummage in my stuff and think you can cross-talk me just cause you call me Daddy? If she told you I was your daddy, then she told you more than she told me. Get a hold of yourself. A son ain't what a woman say. A son is what a man do. You want to act like you mine, then do it, else get the devil out my house!"

"I didn't come down here to court you, get your approval."

"I know what you came for. To see how black I was. You thought you was white, didn't you? She probably let you think it. Hoped you'd think it. And I swear I'd think it too."

"She protected me! If she'd announced I was a nigger, I could have been a slave!"

"They got free niggers. Always did have some free niggers. You could be one of them."

"I don't want to be a free nigger; I want to be a free man."

"Don't we all. Look. Be what you want—white or black. Choose. But if you choose black, you got to act black, meaning draw your manhood up—quicklike, and don't bring me no whiteboy sass."

Golden Gray was sober now and his sober thought was to blow the man's head off. Tomorrow.

It must have been the girl who changed his mind.

Girls can do that. Steer a man away from death or drive him right to it. Pull you out of sleep and you wake up on the ground under a tree you'll never locate again because you're lost. Or if you do find it, it won't be the same. Maybe it cracked from the inside, bored through by crawling life that had to have its own way too, and just crept and bunched and gnawed and burrowed until the whole thing was pitted through with the service it rendered to others. Or maybe they cut it down before it crashed in on itself. Turned it into logs for a fire in a big hearth for children to gaze into.

Victory might remember. He was more than Joe's chosen brother, he was his best friend, and they hunted through and worked in most of Vesper County. Not even a sheriff's map would show the walnut tree Joe fell out of, but Victory would remember it. It could be there still, in somebody's backyard, but the cotton fields and the colored neighborhood around them were churned up and pressed down.

One week of rumors, two days of packing, and nine hundred Negroes, encouraged by guns and hemp, left Vienna, rode out of town on wagons or walked on their feet to who knew (or cared) where. With two days' notice? How can you plan where to go, and if you do know of a place you think will welcome you, where is the money to arrive?

They stood around at the depot, camped in fields on the edge of the road in clusters until shooed away for being the blight that had been visited upon them—for reflecting like still water the disconsolateness they certainly felt, and for reminding others about the wages sin paid out to its laborers.

The cane field where Wild hid, or watched, or laughed out loud, or stayed quiet burned for months. The sugar smell lingered in the smoke—weighting it. Would she know? he wondered. Would she understand that fire was not light or flowers moving toward her, or flying golden hair? That if you tried to touch or kiss it, it would swallow your breath away?

The little graveyards, with handmade crosses and sometimes a stone marker pleading for remembrance in careful block letters, never stood a chance.

Hunter refused to leave; he was more in the woods than in his cabin anyway, and seemed to look forward to spending his last days in the places he felt most comfortable. So he didn't haul his gear to a wagon. Or walk the road to Bear, then Crossland, then Goshen, then Palestine looking for a workplace as Joe and Victory did. Some farm that would give thirteen-year-old black boys space to sleep and food in return for clearing brush. Or a mill that had a bunkhouse. Joe and Victory walked the road along with the others for a while, then took off. They knew they had left Crossland far behind when they passed the walnut tree where they used to sleep on nights when, hunting far from home, cool air could be found high in its branches. And when they looked back down the road, they could still see smoke lifting from what was left of the fields and the cane of Vienna. They found short work at a sawmill in Bear, then an afternoon pulling stumps at Crossland, finally steady work in Goshen. Then one spring the southern third of the county erupted in fat white cotton balls, and Joe left Victory helping the smithy at Goshen for the lucrative crop picking going on outside Palestine, some fifteen miles away. But first, first he had to know if the woman he believed was his mother was still there—or had she confused fire with hair and lost her breath to it.

All in all, he made three solitary journeys to find her. In Vienna he had lived first with the fear of her, then the joke of her, finally the obsession, followed by rejection of her. Nobody told Joe she was his mother. Not outright; but Hunters Hunter looked right in his eyes one evening and said, "She got reasons. Even if she crazy. Crazy people got reasons."

They were cleaning up after eating some of what they'd caught. Joe believed later it was fowl, but it could have been something with fur. Victory would remember. Victory was wiping the roasting stick with leaves while Joe leveled the fire.

"I taught both you all never kill the tender and nothing female if you can help it. Didn't think I had to teach you about people. Now, learn this: she ain't prey. You got to know the difference."

Victory and Joe had been joking, speculating on what it would take to kill Wild if they happened on her. If the trail of her all three of them sometimes saw and followed led straight to her hide. That's when Hunter said it. About how crazy people have reasons. Then he looked right at Joe (not Victory). The low fire galvanized his stare. "You know, that woman is *somebody*'s mother and *somebody* ought to take care."

Victory and Joe exchanged looks, but it was Joe's flesh that cooled and his throat that tried and failed to swallow.

From then on he wrestled with the notion of a wildwoman for a mother. Sometimes it shamed him to tears. Other times his anger messed up his aim and he shot wild or hit game in messy inefficient places. A lot of his time was spent denying it, convincing himself he misread Hunter's words and most of all his look. Nevertheless, Wild was always on his mind, and he wasn't going to leave for Palestine without trying to find her one more time.

She wasn't always in the cane. Nor the back part of the woods on a whiteman's farm. He and Hunter and Victory had seen traces of her in those woods: ruined honeycombs, the bits and leavings of stolen victuals and many times the signal Hunter relied on most—redwings, those blue-black birds with the bolt of red on their wings. Something about her they liked, said Hunter, and seeing four or more of them always meant she was close. Hunter had spoken to her there twice, he said, but Joe knew that those woods were not her favorite place. The first time he'd looked for her it was a halfhearted search after a couple of hours' spectacular fishing. Across the river, beyond the place where the trout and the bass were plentiful but before the river went underground heading for the mill, the bank turned around an incline. On top of it, some fifteen feet above the river was a sheltering rock formation, its entrance blocked by hedges of old hibiscus. Once, after pulling ten trout in the first hour of dawn, Joe had walked past that place and heard what he first believed was some combination of running water and wind in high trees. The music the world makes, familiar to fishermen and shepherds, woodsmen have also heard. It hypnotizes mammals. Bucks raise their heads and gophers freeze. Attentive woodsmen smile and close their eyes.

Joe thought that was it, and simply listened with pleasure until a word or two seemed to glide into the sound. Knowing the music the world makes has no words, he stood rock still and scanned his surroundings. A silver line lay across the opposite bank, sun cutting into the last of the night's royal blue. Above and to his left hibiscus thick, savage and old. Its blossoms were closed waiting for the day. The scrap of song came from a woman's throat, and Joe thrashed and beat his way up the incline and through the hedge, a tangle of muscadine vines, Virginia creeper and hibiscus rusty with age. He found the opening in the rock formation but could not enter it from that angle. He would have to climb above it and slide down into its mouth. The light was so small he could barely see his legs. But he saw tracks enough to know she was there.

He called out. "Anybody there?"

The song stopped, and a snap like the breaking of twigs took its place.

"Hey! You in there!"

Nothing stirred and he could not persuade himself that the fragrance that floated over him was not a mixture of honey and shit. He left then, disgusted, and not a little afraid.

The second time he looked for her was after the dispossession. Having seen the smoke and tasted the sugared air on his tongue, he delayed his journey to Palestine to detour back toward Vienna. Skirting the burned ground and fields of black stalks; looking away from the cabins that were now just hot bricks where a washtub once stood, he headed for the river and the hole in it where trout multiplied like flies. When he reached the place where the river turned he adjusted the rifle strapped to his back and dropped to his haunches.

Slowly, breathing softly through his mouth, he crawled toward the rocks shut away by greenery grown ruthless in sun and air. There was no sign of her, nothing he recognized. He managed to climb above the opening, but when he slid down and entered the rock place, he saw nothing a woman could use and the vestiges of human habitation were cold. Had she run away, escaped? Or had she been overtaken by smoke, fire, panic, helplessness? Joe waited there, till his listening made him drowsy and he slept for an hour or more. When he woke the day had moved and the hibiscus was as wide as his hand. He hauled himself down the incline and, as he turned to go four redwings shot up from the lower limbs of a white-oak tree. Huge, isolated, it grew in unlikely soil—entwined in its own roots. Immediately Joe fell to his hands and knees, whispering: "Is it you? Just say it. Say anything." Someone near him was breathing. Turning round he examined the place he had just exited. Every movement and leaf shift seemed to be her. "Give me a sign, then. You don't have to say nothing. Let me see your hand. Just stick it out someplace and I'll go; I promise. A sign." He begged, pleaded for her hand until the light grew even smaller. "You my mother?" Yes. No. Both. Either. But not this nothing.

Whispering into hibiscus stalks and listening to breathing, he suddenly saw himself pawing around in the dirt for a not just crazy but also dirty woman who happened to be his secret mother that Hunter once knew but who orphaned her baby rather than nurse him or coddle him or stay in the house with him. A woman who frightened children, made men sharpen knives, for whom brides left food out (might as well—otherwise she stole it). Leaving traces of her sloven unhousebroken self all over the county. Shaming him before everybody but Victory, who neither laughed nor slant-eyed him when Joe told him what he believed Hunter meant by those words and especially that look. "She must be tough" was Victory's reply. "Live outside like that all year round, she must be tough."

Maybe so, but right then Joe felt like a lint-headed fool, crazier than she and just as wild as he slipped into mud, tripped over black roots, scuffed through patches of dirt crawling with termites. He loved the woods because Hunter taught him how to. But now they were full of her, a simple-minded woman too silly to beg for a living. Too brain-blasted to do what the meanest sow managed: nurse what she birthed. The small children believed she was a witch, but they were wrong. This creature hadn't the intelligence to be a witch. She was powerless, invisible, wastefully daft. Everywhere and nowhere.

There are boys who have whores for mothers and don't get over it. There are boys whose mothers stagger through town roads when the juke joint slams its door. Mothers who throw their children away or trade them for folding money. He would have chosen any one of them over this indecent speechless lurking insanity. The blast he aimed at the white-oak limbs disturbed nothing, for the shells were in his pocket. The trigger clicked harmlessly. Yelling, sliding, falling, he raced back down the incline and followed the riverbank out of there.

From then on his work was maniacal. On his way to Palestine, he took every job offered or heard about. Cut trees, cane; plowed till he could hardly lift his arms; plucked chickens and cotton; hauled lumber, grain, quarry rocks and stock. Some thought he was money hungry, but others guessed that Joe didn't like to be still or thought of as lazy. Sometimes he worked so long and late he never got back to the bed he bunked in. Then he would sleep outside, sometimes lucky enough to be near the walnut tree; swinging in the tarp they kept there for when they needed it. After Palestine, when the cotton was in, baled and spoken for, Joe got married and worked even harder.

Did Hunter stay near Vienna after the fire? Move back to Wordsworth? Fix himself a little place up country—like he talked of doing—and work the world his own way? In 1926, far away from all those places, Joe thought maybe it was Wordsworth Hunter moved near to, and if he could ask him, Victory would remember exactly (assuming he was alive and prison had not rattled him) because Victory remembered everything and could keep things clear in his mind. Like how many times peahens had used a certain nest. Like where a henna carpet of pine needles was shin-bone deep. Like whether a particular tree—the one whose roots grew up its trunk—was in bud two days ago or a week and exactly where it was.

Joe is wondering about all this on an icy day in January. He is a long way from Virginia, and even longer from Eden. As he puts on his coat and cap he can practically feel Victory at his side when he sets out, armed, to find Dorcas. He isn't thinking of harming her, or, as Hunter had cautioned, killing something tender. She is female. And she is not prey. So he never thinks of that. He is hunting for her though, and while hunting a gun is as natural a companion as Victory.

He stalks through the City and it does not object or interfere. It's the first day of the year. Most people are tired from the night before. Colored people, however, are still celebrating with a day gathering, a feast that can linger into the night. The streets are slippery. The City looks as uninhabited as a small town.

"I just want to see her. Tell her I know she didn't mean what she said. She's young. Young people fly off the handle. Bust out just for the hell of it. Like me shooting an unloaded shotgun at the leaves that time. Like me saying, 'All right, Violet, I'll marry you,' just because I couldn't see whether a wildwoman put out her hand or not."

The streets he walks are slick and black. In his coat pocket is the forty-five he pawned his rifle for. He had laughed when he handled it, a fat baby gun that would be loud as a cannon. Nothing complex; you'd have to fight your own self to miss, but he isn't going to miss because he isn't going to aim. Not at that insulted skin. Never. Never hurt the young: nest eggs, roe, fledglings, fry . . .

A wind rips up from the mouth of the tunnel and blows his cap off. He runs to get it from the gutter it swept into. He doesn't see the paper ring from a White Owl cigar that sticks to the crown of his cap. Once inside the train he perspires heavily and takes off his coat. The paper sack thuds to the floor. Joe looks down at the fingers of a passenger who reaches for the bag and returns it to him. Joe nods a thank you and shoves the sack back into his coat pocket. A Negro woman shakes her head at him. At the paper sack? Its contents? No, at his dripping face. She holds out to him a fresh handkerchief to wipe it. He refuses; puts his coat back on and moves to the door to stare into the swiftness and the dark.

The train stops suddenly, throwing passengers forward. As though it just remembered that this was the stop where Joe needs to get off if he is going to find her.

Three girls pile out of the train and clack down the icy stairs. Three waiting men greet them and they all pair off. It is biting cold. The girls have red lips and their legs whisper to each other through silk stockings. The red lips and the silk flash power. A power they will exchange for the right to be overcome, penetrated. The men at their side love it because, in the end, they will reach in, extend, get back behind that power, grab it and keep it still.

The third time Joe had tried to find her (he was a married man by then) he had searched the hillside for the tree—the one whose roots grew backward as though, having gone obediently into earth and found it barren, retreating to the trunk for what was needed. Defiant and against logic its roots climbed. Toward leaves, light, wind. Below that tree was the river whites called Treason where fish raced to the line, and swimming among them could be riotous or serene. But to get there you risked treachery by the very ground you walked on. The slopes and low hills that fell gently toward the river only appeared welcoming; underneath vines, carpet grass, wild grape, hibiscus and wood sorrel, the ground was as porous as a sieve. A step could swallow your foot or your whole self.

"What would she want with a rooster? Crowing on a corner, looking at the chickens to pick over them. Nothing they have I don't have better. Plus I know how to treat a woman. I never have, never would, mistreat one. Never would make a woman live like a dog in a cave. The roosters would. She used to say that too. How the young ones couldn't think about anybody but themselves; how in the playground or at a dance all those boys thought about was themselves. When I find her, I know—I bet my life—she won't be holed up with one of them. His clothes won't be all mixed up with hers. Not her. Not Dorcas. She'll be alone. Hardheaded. Wild, even. But alone."

• • •

Beyond the tree, behind the hibiscus, was a boulder. Behind it an opening so badly disguised it could be only the work of a human. No fox or foaling doe would be so sloppy. Had she been hiding there? Was she that small? He squatted to look closer for signs of her, recognizing none. Finally he stuck his head in. Pitch dark. No odor of dung or fur. It had, instead, a domestic smell—oil, ashes—that led him on. Crawling, squirming through a space low enough to graze his hair. Just as he decided to back out of there, the dirt under his hands became stone and light hit him so hard he flinched. He had come through a few body-lengths of darkness and was looking out the south side of the rock face. A natural burrow. Going nowhere. Angling through one curve of the slope to another. Treason River glistening below. Unable to turn around inside, he pulled himself all the way out to reenter head first. Immediately he was in open air the domestic smell intensified. Cooking oil reeked under stabbing sunlight. Then he saw the crevice. He went into it on his behind until a floor stopped his slide. It was like falling into the sun. Noon light followed him like lava into a stone room where somebody cooked in oil.

"She don't have to explain. She don't have to say a word. I know how it is. She might think it's jealousy, but I'm a mild man. It's not that I don't feel things. I've known some tough times. Got through them, too. I feel things just like everybody else.

"She'll be all alone.

"She'll turn to me.

"She will hold out her hand, walk toward me in ugly shoes, but her face is clean and I am proud of her. Her too-tight braids torture her so she unlooses them as she moves toward me. She's so glad I found her. Arching and soft, wanting me to do it, asking me to. Just me. Nobody but me."

He felt peace at the beginning, and a kind of watchfulness, as though something waited. A before-supper feeling when someone waits to eat. Although it was a private place, with an opening closed to the public, once inside you could do what you pleased: disrupt things, rummage, touch and move. Change it all to a way it was never meant to be. The color of the stone walls had changed from gold to fish-gill blue by the time he left. He had seen what there was. A green dress. A rocking chair without an arm. A circle of stones for cooking. Jars, baskets, pots; a doll, a spindle, earrings, a photograph, a stack of sticks, a set of silver brushes and a silver cigar case. Also. Also, a pair of man's trousers with buttons of bone. Carefully folded, a silk shirt, faded pale and creamy—except at the seams. There, both thread and fabric were a fresh and sunny yellow.

But where is *she?*

There she is. No dancing brothers are in this place, nor any breathless girls waiting for the white bulb to be exchanged for the blue. This is an adult party—what goes on goes on in bright light. The illegal liquor is not secret and the secrets are not forbidden. Pay a dollar or two when you enter and what you say is smarter, funnier, than it would be in your own kitchen. Your wit surfaces over and over like the rush of foam to the rim. The laughter is like pealing bells that don't need a hand to pull on the rope; it just goes on and on until you are weak with it. You can drink the safe gin if you like, or stick to beer, but you don't need either because a touch on the knee, accidental or on purpose, alerts the blood like a shot of pre-Pro bourbon or two fingers pinching your nipple. Your spirit lifts to the ceiling where it floats for a bit looking down with pleasure on the dressed-up nakedness below. You know something wicked is going on in a room with a closed door. But there is enough dazzle and mischief here, where partners cling or exchange at the urging of a heartbreaking vocal.

Dorcas is satisfied, content. Two arms clasp her and she is able to rest her cheek on her own shoulder while her wrists cross behind his neck. It's good they don't need much space to dance in because there isn't any. The room is packed. Men groan their satisfaction; women hum anticipation. The music bends, falls to its knees to embrace them all, encourage them all to live a little, why don't you? since this is the it you've been looking for.

Her partner does not whisper in Dorcas' ear. His promises are already clear in the chin he presses into her hair, the fingertips that stay. She stretches up to encircle his neck. He bends to help her do it. They agree on everything above the waist and below: muscle, tendon, bone joint and marrow cooperate. And if the dancers hesitate, have a moment of doubt, the music will solve and dissolve any question.

Dorcas is happy. Happier than she has ever been anytime. No white strands grow in her partner's mustache. He is up and coming. Hawk-eyed, tireless and a little cruel. He has never given her a present or even thought about it. Sometimes he is where he says he will be; sometimes not. Other women want him—badly—and he has been selective. What they want and the prize it is his to give is his savvy self. What could a pair of silk stockings be compared to him? No contest. Dorcas is lucky. Knows it. And is as happy as she has ever been anytime.

. . .

"He is coming for me. I know he is because I know how flat his eyes went when I told him not to. And how they raced afterward. I didn't say it nicely, although I meant to. I practiced the points; in front of the mirror I went through them one by one: the sneaking around, and his wife and all. I never said anything about our ages or Acton. Nothing about Acton. But he argued with me so I said, Leave me alone. Just leave me alone. Get away from me. You bring me another bottle of cologne I'll drink it and die you don't leave me alone.

"He said, You can't die from cologne.

"I said, You know what I mean.

"He said, You want me to leave my wife?

"I said, No! I want you to leave *me.* I don't want you inside me. I don't want you beside me. I hate this room. I don't want to be here and don't come looking for me.

"He said, Why?

"I said, Because. Because. Because.

"He said, Because what?

"I said, Because you make me sick.

"Sick? I make you sick?

"Sick of myself and sick of you.

"I didn't mean that part . . . about being sick. He didn't. Make me sick, I mean. What I wanted to let him know was that I had this chance to have Acton and I wanted it and I wanted girlfriends to talk to about it. About where we went and what he did. About things. About stuff. What good are secrets if you can't talk to anybody about them? I sort of hinted about Joe and me to Felice and she laughed before she stared at me and then frowned.

"I couldn't tell him all that because I had practiced the other points and got mixed up.

"But he's coming for me. I know it. He's been looking for me all over. Maybe tomorrow he'll find me. Maybe tonight. Way out here; all the way out here.

"When we got off the streetcar, me and Acton and Felice, I thought he was there in the doorway next to the candy store, but it wasn't him. Not yet. I think I see him everywhere. I know he's looking and now I know he's coming.

"He didn't even care what I looked like. I could be anything, do anything—and it pleased him. Something about that made me mad. I don't know.

"Acton, now, he tells me when he doesn't like the way I fix my hair. Then I do it how he likes it. I never wear glasses when he is with me and I changed my laugh for him to one he likes better. I think he does. I know he didn't like it before. And I play with my food now. Joe liked for me to eat it all up and want more. Acton gives me a quiet look when I ask for seconds. He worries about me that way. Joe never did. Joe didn't care what kind of woman I was. He should have. I cared. I wanted to have a personality and with Acton I'm getting one. I have a look now. What pencil-thin eyebrows do for my face is a dream. All my bracelets are just below my elbow. Sometimes I knot my stockings below, not above, my knees. Three straps are across my instep and at home I have shoes with leather cut out to look like lace.

"He is coming for me. Maybe tonight. Maybe here.

"If he does he will look and see how close me and Acton dance. How I rest my head on my arm holding on to him. The hem of my skirt drapes down in back and taps the calves of my legs while we rock back and forth, then side to side. The whole front of us touches. Nothing can get between us we are so close. Lots of girls here want to be doing this with him. I can see them when I open my eyes to look past his neck. I rub my thumbnail over his nape so the girls will know I know they want him. He doesn't like it and turns his head to make me stop touching his neck that way. I stop.

"Joe wouldn't care. I could rub anywhere on him. He let me draw lipstick pictures in places he had to have a mirror to see."

Anything that happens after this party breaks up is nothing. Everything is now. It's like war. Everyone is handsome, shining just thinking about other people's blood. As though the red wash flying from veins not theirs is facial makeup patented for its glow. Inspiriting. Glamorous. Afterward there will be some chatter and recapitulation of what went on; nothing though like the action itself and the beat that pumps the heart. In war or at a party everyone is wily, intriguing; goals are set and altered; alliances rearranged. Partners and rivals devastated; new pairings triumphant. The knockout possibilities knock Dorcas out because here—with grown-ups and as in war—people play for keeps.

"He is coming for me. And when he does he will see I'm not his anymore. I'm Acton's and it's Acton I want to please. He expects it. With Joe I pleased myself because he encouraged me to. With Joe I worked the stick of the world, the power in my hand."

• • •

Oh, the room—the music—the people leaning in doorways. Silhouettes kiss behind curtains; playful fingers examine and caress. This is the place where things pop. This is the market where gesture is all: a tongue's lightning lick; a thumbnail grazing the split cheeks of a purple plum. Any thrownaway lover in wet unlaced shoes and a buttoned-up sweater under his coat is a foreigner here. This is not the place for old men; this is the place for romance.

"He's here. Oh, look. God. He's crying. Am I falling? Why am I falling? Acton is holding me up but I am falling anyway. Heads are turning to look where I am falling. It's dark and now it's light. I am lying on a bed. Somebody is wiping sweat from my forehead, but I am cold, so cold. I see mouths moving; they are all saying something to me I can't hear. Way out there at the foot of the bed I see Acton. Blood is on his coat jacket and he is dabbing at it with a white handkerchief. Now a woman takes the coat from his shoulders. He is annoyed by the blood. It's my blood, I guess, and it has stained through his jacket to his shirt. The hostess is shouting. Her party is ruined. Acton looks angry; the woman brings his jacket back and it is not clean the way it was before and the way he likes it.

"I can hear them now.

" 'Who? Who did this?'

"I'm tired. Sleepy. I ought to be wide awake because something important is happening.

" 'Who did this, girl? Who did this to you?'

"They want me to say his name. Say it in public at last.

"Acton has taken his shirt off. People are blocking the doorway; some stretch behind them to get a better look. The record playing is over. Somebody they have been waiting for is playing the piano. A woman is singing too. The music is faint but I know the words by heart.

"Felice leans close. Her hand holding mine is too tight. I try to say with my mouth to come nearer. Her eyes are bigger than the light fixture on the ceiling. She asks me was it him.

"They need me to say his name so they can go after him. Take away his sample case with Rochelle and Bernadine and Faye inside. I know his name but Mama won't tell. The world rocked from a stick beneath my hand, Felice. There in that room with the ice sign in the window.

"Felice puts her ear on my lips and I scream it to her. I think I am screaming it. I think I am.

"People are leaving.

"Now it's clear. Through the doorway I see the table. On it is a brown wooden bowl, flat, low like a tray, full to spilling with oranges. I want to sleep, but it is clear now. So clear the dark bowl the pile of oranges. Just oranges. Bright. Listen. I don't know who is that woman singing but I know the words by heart."

Sweetheart. That's what that weather was called. Sweetheart weather, the prettiest day of the year. And that's when it started. On a day so pure and steady trees preened. Standing in the middle of a concrete slab, scared for their lives, they preened. Silly, yes, but it was that kind of day. I could see Lenox widening itself, and men coming out of their shops to look at it, to stand with their hands under their aprons or stuck in their back pockets and just look around at a street that spread itself wider to hold the day. Disabled veterans in half uniform and half civilian stopped looking gloomy at workingmen; they went to Father Divine's wagon and after they'd eaten they rolled cigarettes and settled down on the curb as though it were a Duncan Phyfe. And the women tip-tapping their heels on the pavement tripped sometimes on the sidewalk cracks because they were glancing at the trees to see where that pure, soft but steady light was coming from. The rumbling of the M11 and M2 was distant, far away and the Packards too. Even those loud Fords quieted down, and no one felt like blowing his horn or leaning out the driver's side to try and embarrass somebody taking too long to cross the street. The sweetness of the day tickled them, made them holler "I give you everything I got! you come home with me!" to a woman tripping in shiny black heels over the cracks.

Young men on the rooftops changed their tune; spit and fiddled with the mouthpiece for a while and when they put it back in and blew out their cheeks it was just like the light of that day, pure and steady and kind of kind. You would have thought everything had been forgiven the way they played. The clarinets had trouble because the brass was cut so fine, not lowdown the way they love to do it, but high and fine like a young girl singing by the side of a creek, passing the time, her ankles cold in the water. The young men with brass probably never saw such a girl, or such a creek, but they made her up that day. On the rooftops. Some on 254 where there is no protective railing; another at 131, the one with the apple-green water tank, and somebody right next to it, 133, where lard cans of tomato plants are kept, and a pallet for sleeping at night. To find coolness and a way to avoid mosquitoes unable to fly that high up or unwilling to leave the tender neck meat near the street lamps. So from Lenox to St. Nicholas and across 135th Street, Lexington, from Convent to Eighth I could hear the men playing out their maple-sugar hearts, tapping it from four-hundred-year-old trees and letting it run down the trunk, wasting it because they didn't have a bucket to hold it and didn't want one either. They just wanted to let it run that day, slow if it wished, or fast, but a free run down trees bursting to give it up.

That's the way the young men on brass sounded that day. Sure of themselves, sure they were holy, standing up there on the rooftops, facing each other at first, but when it was clear that they had beat the clarinets out, they turned their backs on them, lifted those horns straight up and joined the light just as pure and steady and kind of kind.

No day to wreck a life already splintered like a cheap windowpane, but Violet, well you had to know Violet. She thought all she had to do was drink malts full of Dr. Dee's Nerve and Flesh Builder, eat pork, and she'd put on enough weight to fill out the back of her dress. She usually wore a coat on warm days like this to keep the men at curbside from shaking their heads in pity when she walked by. But on this day, this kind, pretty day, she didn't care about her missing behind because she came out the door and stood on the porch with her elbows in her hands and her stockings rolled down to her ankles. She had been listening to the music penetrate Joe's sobs, which were quieter now. Probably because she had returned Dorcas' photograph to Alice Manfred. But the space where the photo had been was real. Perhaps that's why, standing there on the porch, unmindful of her behind, she easily believed that what was coming up the steps toward her was another true-as-life Dorcas, four marcelled waves and all.

She carried an Okeh record under her arm and a half pound of stewmeat wrapped in pink butcher paper in her hand although the sun is too hot to linger in the streets with meat. If she doesn't hurry it will turn—cook itself before she can get it to the stove.

Lazy girl. Her arms are full but there is nothing much in her head.

She makes me nervous.

She makes me wonder if this fine weather will last more than a day. I am already disturbed by the ash falling from the blue distance down on these streets. A sooty film is gathering on the sills, coating the windowpanes. Now she is disturbing me, making me doubt my own self just looking at her sauntering through the sunshafts like that. Climbing the steps now, heading for Violent.

"My mother and my father too lived in Tuxedo. I almost never saw them. I lived with my grandmother who said, 'Felice, they don't live in Tuxedo; they work there and live with us.' Just words: live, work. I would see them once every three weeks for two and a half days, and all day Christmas and all day Easter. I counted. Forty-two days if you count the half days—which I don't, because most of it was packing and getting to the train—plus two holidays makes forty-four days, but really only thirty-four because the half days shouldn't count. Thirty-four days a year.

"When they'd come home, they'd kiss me and give me things, like my opal ring, but what they really wanted to do was go out dancing somewhere (my mother) or sleep (my father). They made it to church on the Sunday, but my mother is still sad about that because all of the things she should have been doing in the church—the suppers, the meetings, the fixing up of the basement for Sunday-school parties and the receptions after funerals—she had to say no to, because of her job in Tuxedo. So more than anything she wanted gossip from the women in Circle A Society about what'd been going on; and she wanted to dance a little and play bid whist.

"My father preferred to stay in a bathrobe and be waited on for a change while he read the stacks of newspapers me and my grandmother saved for him. The *Amsterdam,* the *Age, The Crisis, The Messenger,* the *Worker.* Some he took back with him to Tuxedo because he couldn't get them up there. He likes them folded properly if they are newspapers, and no food or fingerprints on the magazines, so I don't read them much. My grandmother does and is very very careful not to wrinkle or soil them. Nothing makes him madder than to open a paper that is badly folded. He groans and grunts while he reads and once in a while he laughs, but he'd never give it up even though all that reading worries his blood, my grandmother said. The good part for him is to read everything and argue about what he's read with my mother and grandmother and the friends they play cards with.

"Once I thought if I read the papers we'd saved I could argue with him. But I picked wrong. I read about the white policemen who were arrested for killing some Negroes and said I was glad they were arrested, that it was about time.

"He looked at me and shouted, 'The story hit the paper because it was news, girl, news!'

"I didn't know how to answer him and started to cry so my grandmother said, 'Sonny, go somewhere and sit down,' and my mother said, 'Walter, shut up about all that to her.'

"She explained to me what he meant: that for the everyday killings cops did of Negroes, nobody was arrested at all. She took me shopping after that for some things her bosses in Tuxedo wanted, and I didn't ask her why she had to shop for them on her off days, because then she wouldn't have taken me to Tiffany's on Thirty-seventh Street where it's quieter than when Reverend asks for a minute of silent prayer. When that happens I can hear feet scraping and some people blow their noses. But in Tiffany's nobody blows a nose and the carpet prevents shoe noises of any kind. Like Tuxedo.

"Years ago when I was little, before I started school, my parents would take me there. I had to be quiet all the time. Twice they took me and I stayed the whole three weeks. It stopped, though. My mother and father talked about quitting but they didn't. They got my grandmother to move in and watch over me.

"Thirty-four days. I'm seventeen now and that works out to less than six hundred days. Less than two years out of seventeen. Dorcas said I was lucky because at least they were there, somewhere, and if I got sick I could call on them or get on the train and go see them. Both of her parents died in a very bad way and she saw them after they died and before the funeral men fixed them up. She had a photograph of them sitting under a painted palm tree. Her mother was standing up with her hand on the father's shoulder. He was sitting down and holding a book. They looked sad to me, but Dorcas couldn't get over how good looking they both were.

"She was always talking about who was good looking and who wasn't. Who had bad breath, who had nice clothes, who could dance, who was hincty.

"My grandmother was suspicious of us being friends. She never said why but I sort of knew. I didn't have a lot of friends in school. Not the boys but the girls in my school bunched off according to their skin color. I hate that stuff—Dorcas too. So me and her were different that way. When some nastymouth hollered, 'Hey, fly, where's buttermilk?' or 'Hey, kinky, where's kind?' we stuck our tongues out and put our fingers in our noses to shut them up. But if that didn't work we'd lay into them. Some of those fights ruined my clothes and Dorcas' glasses, but it felt good fighting those girls with Dorcas. She was never afraid and we had the best times. Every school we went to, every day.

"It stopped, the good times, for a couple of months when she started seeing that old man. I knew about it from the start, but she didn't know I did. I let her think it was a secret because she wanted it to be one. At first I thought she was shamed of it, or shamed of him and was just in it for the presents. But she liked secret stuff. Planning and plotting how to deceive Mrs. Manfred. Slipping vampy underwear on at my house to go walking in. Hiding things. She always did like secrets. She wasn't ashamed of him either.

"He's old. Really old. Fifty. But he met her standards of good looking, I'll say that for him. Dorcas should have been prettier than she was. She just missed. She had all the ingredients of pretty too. Long hair, wavy, half good, half bad. Light skinned. Never used skin bleach. Nice shape. But it missed somehow. If you looked at each thing, you would admire that thing—the hair, the color, the shape. All together it didn't fit. Guys looked at her, whistled and called out fresh stuff when we walked down the street. In school all sorts of boys wanted to talk to her. But then they stopped; nothing came of it. It couldn't have been her personality because she was a good talker, liked to joke and tease. Nothing standoffish about her. I don't know what it was. Unless it was the way she pushed them. I mean it was like she wanted them to do something scary all the time. Steal things, or go back in the store and slap the face of a white salesgirl who wouldn't wait on her, or cuss out somebody who had snubbed her. Beats me. Everything was like a picture show to her, and she was the one on the railroad track, or the one trapped in the sheik's tent when it caught on fire.

"I think that's what made her like that old man so much at first. The secrecy and that he had a wife. He must have done something dangerous when she first met him or she would never have gone on sneaking around with him. Anyway, she thought she was sneaking. But two hairdressers saw her in that nightclub, Mexico, with him. I spent two hours in there listening to what they had to say about her and him and all kinds of other people who were stepping out. They had fun talking about Dorcas and him mostly because they didn't like his wife. She took away their trade, so they had nothing good to say about her, except crazy as she was she did do hair well and if she wasn't so crazy she could have got a license proper instead of taking away their trade.

"They're wrong about her. I went to look for my ring and there is nothing crazy about her at all.

"I know my mother stole that ring. She said her boss lady gave it to her, but I remember it in Tiffany's that day. A silver ring with a smooth black stone called opal. The salesgirl went to get the package my mother came to pick up. She showed the girl the note from her boss lady so they would give it to her (and even showed it at the door, so they would let her in). While the salesgirl was gone, we looked at the velvet tray of rings. Picked some up and tried to try them on, but a man in a beautiful suit came over and shook his head. Very slightly.

'I'm waiting for a package for Mrs. Nicolson,' my mother said.

"The man smiled then and said, 'Of course. It's just policy. We have to be careful.' When we left my mother said, 'Of what? What does he have to be careful about? They put the tray out so people can look at the things, don't they? So what does he have to be careful about?'

"She frowned and fussed and we waited a long time for a taxi to take us home and she dared my father to say something about it. The next morning, they packed and got ready to take the train back to Tuxedo Junction. She called me over and gave me the ring she said her boss lady had given her. Maybe they made lots of them, but I know my mother took it from the velvet tray. Out of spite, I suppose, but she gave it to me and I love it, and only lent it to Dorcas because she begged so hard and the silver of it did match the bracelets at her elbow.

"She wanted to impress Acton. A hard job since he criticized everything. He never gave her gifts the way the old man did. I know she took stuff from him because Mrs. Manfred would die before she bought slippery underwear or silk stockings for Dorcas. Things she couldn't wear at home or to church.

"After Dorcas picked up with Acton, we saw each other like before, but she was different. She was doing for Acton what the old man did for her—giving him little presents she bought from the money she wheedled out of the old man and from Mrs. Manfred. Nobody ever caught Dorcas looking for work, but she worked hard scheming money to give Acton things. Stuff he didn't like, anyway, because it was cheap, and he never wore that ugly stickpin or the silk handkerchief either because of the color. I guess the old man taught her how to be nice, and she wasted it on Acton, who took it for granted, and took her for granted and any girl who liked him.

"I don't know if she quit the old man or just two-timed him with Acton. My grandmother says she brought it on herself. Live the life; pay the price, she said.

"I have to get on home. If I sit here too long, some man will think I'm looking for a good time. Not anymore. After what happened to Dorcas, all I want is my ring back. To have and to show my mother I still have it. She asks me about it once in a while. She's sick and doesn't work in Tuxedo anymore, and my father has a job on the Pullman. He is happier than I've ever seen him. When he reads the papers and magazines he still grunts and talks back to the printed words, but he gets them first and freshly folded and his arguments aren't so loud. 'I've seen the world now,' he says.

"He means Tuxedo and the train stops in Pennsylvania and Ohio and Indiana and Illinois. 'And all the kinds of white-people there are. Two kinds,' he says. 'The ones that feel sorry for you and the ones that don't. And both amount to the same thing. Nowhere in between is respect.'

"He's as argumentative as ever, but happier because riding trains he gets to see Negroes play baseball 'in the flesh and on the lot, goddamnit.' It tickles him that whitepeople are scared to compete with Negroes fair and square.

"My grandmother is slower now, and my mother is sick, so I do most of the cooking. My mother wants me to find some good man to marry. I want a good job first. Make my own money. Like she did. Like Mrs. Trace. Like Mrs. Manfred used to before Dorcas let herself die.

"I stopped in there to see if he had my ring, because my mother kept asking me about it, and because I couldn't find it when I rummaged around in Mrs. Manfred's house after the funeral. But I had another reason too. The hairdresser said the old man was all broke up. Cried all day and all night. Left his job and wasn't good for a thing. I suppose he misses Dorcas, and thinks about how he is her murderer. But he must not have known about her. How she liked to push people, men. All except Acton, but she would have pushed him too if she had lived long enough or if he had stayed around long enough. It was just for attention or the excitement. I was there at the party and I was the one she talked to on the bed.

"I thought about it for three months and when I heard he was still at it, crying and so on, I made up my mind to tell him about her. About what she said to me. So on my way home from the market, I stopped by Felton's to get the record my mother wanted. I walked by the building on Lenox where Dorcas used to meet him, and there on the porch was the woman they call Violent because of what they said she did at Dorcas' funeral.

"I didn't go to the funeral. I saw her die like a fool and was too mad to be at her funeral. I didn't go to the viewing either. I hated her after that. Anybody would. Some friend she turned out to be.

"All I wanted was my ring, and to tell the old man he could stop carrying on so. I wasn't afraid of his wife because Mrs. Manfred let her visit and they seemed to get on okay. Knowing how strict Mrs. Manfred was, all the people she said she would never let in her house and that Dorcas should never speak to, I figured if Violent was good enough for her to let in, she was good enough for me to not be afraid of.

"I can see why Mrs. Manfred let her visit. She doesn't lie, Mrs. Trace. Nothing she says is a lie the way it is with most older people. Almost the first thing she said about Dorcas was, 'She was ugly. Outside and in.'

"Dorcas was my friend, but I knew that in a way she was right. All those ingredients of pretty and the recipe didn't work. Mrs. Trace, I thought, was just jealous. She herself is very very dark, bootblack, the girls at school would say. And I didn't expect her to be pretty, but she is. You'd never get tired looking at her face. She's what my grandmother calls pick thin, and wears her hair straightened and flat, slicked back like a man's except that style is all the rage now. Nicely trimmed above her ears and at the kitchen part too. I think her husband must have done her kitchen for her. Who else? She never stepped foot in a beauty shop or so the hairdressers said. I could picture her husband doing her neckline for her. The clippers, maybe even a razor, then the powder afterward. He was that kind, and I sort of know what Dorcas was talking about while she was bleeding all over that woman's bed at the party.

"Dorcas was a fool, but when I met the old man I sort of understood. He has a way about him. And he is handsome. For an old man, I mean. Nothing flabby on him. Nice-shaped head, carries himself like he's somebody. Like my father when he's being a proud Pullman porter seeing the world, and baseball and not cooped up in Tuxedo Junction. But his eyes are not cold like my father's. Mr. Trace looks at you. He has double eyes. Each one a different color. A sad one that lets you look inside him, and a clear one that looks inside you. I like when he looks at me. I feel, I don't know, interesting. He looks at me and I feel deep—as though the things I feel and think are important and different and . . . interesting.

"I think he likes women, and I don't know anybody like that. I don't mean he flirts with them, I mean he likes them without that, and, this would upset the hairdressers, but I really believe he likes his wife.

"When I first went there he was sitting by the window

staring down in the alleyway, not saying anything. Later on Mrs. Trace brought him a plate full of old-people food: vegetable stuff with rice and the cornbread right on top. He said, 'Thank you, baby. Take half for yourself.' Something about the way he said it. As though he appreciated it. When my father says thanks, it's just a word. Mr. Trace acted like he meant it. And when he leaves the room and walks past his wife, he touches her. Sometimes on the head. Sometimes just a pat on her shoulder.

"I've seen him smile twice now and laugh out loud once. Then nobody would know how old he is. He's like a kid when he laughs. But I had visited them three or four times before I ever saw him smile. And that was when I said animals in a zoo were happier than when they were left free because they were safe from hunters. He didn't comment; he just smiled as though what I said was new or really funny.

"That's why I went back. The first time was to see if he had my ring or knew where it was, and to tell him to stop carrying on about Dorcas because maybe she wasn't worth it. The next time, when Mrs. Trace invited me to supper, was more to watch how he was and to listen to Mrs. Trace talk the way she did. A way that would always get her into trouble.

" 'I messed up my own life,' she told me. 'Before I came North I made sense and so did the world. We didn't have nothing but we didn't miss it.'

"Who ever heard of that? Living in the City was the best thing in the world. What can you do out in the country? When I visited Tuxedo, back when I was a child, even then I was bored. How many trees can you look at? That's what I said to her. 'How many trees can you look at? And for how long and so what?'

"She said it wasn't like that, looking at a bunch of trees. She said for me to go to 143rd Street and look at the big one on the corner and see if it was a man or a woman or a child.

"I laughed but before I could agree with the hairdressers that she was crazy, she said, 'What's the world for if you can't make it up the way you want it?'

" 'The way I want it?'

" 'Yeah. The way you want it. Don't you want it to be something more than what it is?'

" 'What's the point? I can't change it.'

" 'That's the point. If you don't, it will change you and it'll be your fault cause you let it. I let it. And messed up my life.'

" 'Messed it up how?'

" 'Forgot it.'

" 'Forgot?'

" 'Forgot it was mine. My life. I just ran up and down the streets wishing I was somebody else.'

" 'Who? Who'd you want to be?'

" 'Not who so much as what. White. Light. Young again.'

" 'Now you don't?'

" 'Now I want to be the woman my mother didn't stay around long enough to see. That one. The one she would have liked and the one I used to like before. . . . My grandmother fed me stories about a little blond child. He was a boy, but I thought of him as a girl sometimes, as a brother, sometimes as a boyfriend. He lived inside my mind. Quiet as a mole. But I didn't know it till I got here. The two of us. Had to get rid of it.'

"She talked like that. But I understood what she meant. About having another you inside that isn't anything like you. Dorcas and I used to make up love scenes and describe them to each other. It was fun and a little smutty. Something about it bothered me, though. Not the loving stuff, but the picture

I had of myself when I did it. Nothing like me. I saw myself as somebody I'd seen in a picture show or a magazine. Then it would work. If I pictured myself the way I am it seemed wrong.

" 'How did you get rid of her?'

" 'Killed her. Then I killed the me that killed her.'

" 'Who's left?'

" 'Me.'

"I didn't say anything. I started thinking maybe the hairdresser was right again because of the way she looked when she said 'me.' Like it was the first she heard of the word.

"Mr. Trace came back in then, and said he was going to sit outside awhile. She said, 'No, Joe. Stay with us. She won't bite.'

"She meant me, and something else I couldn't catch. He nodded and sat down by the window saying, 'For a little while.'

"Mrs. Trace looked at him but I knew she was talking to me when she said, 'Your little ugly friend hurt him and you remind him of her.'

"I could hardly find my tongue. 'I'm not like her!'

"I didn't mean to say it so loud. They both turned to look at me. So I said it even though I didn't plan to. I told them even before I asked for the ring. 'Dorcas let herself die. The bullet went in her shoulder, this way.' I pointed. 'She wouldn't let anybody move her; said she wanted to sleep and she would be all right. Said she'd go to the hospital in the morning. "Don't let them call nobody," she said. "No ambulance; no police, no nobody." I thought she didn't want her aunt, Mrs. Manfred, to know. Where she was and all. And the woman giving the party said okay because she was afraid to call the police. They all were. People just stood around talking and waiting. Some of them wanted to carry her downstairs, put her in a car and drive to the emergency ward. Dorcas said no. She said she was all right. To please leave her alone and let her rest. But I did it. Called the ambulance, I mean; but it didn't come until morning after I had called twice. The ice, they said, but really because it was colored people calling. She bled to death all through that woman's bed sheets on into the mattress, and I can tell you that woman didn't like it one bit. That's all she talked about. Her and Dorcas' boyfriend. The blood. What a mess it made. That's all they talked about.'

"I had to stop then because I was out of breath and crying.

"I hated crying all over myself like that.

"They didn't stop me neither. Mr. Trace handed me his pocket handkerchief, and it was soaked by the time I was through.

" 'This the first time?' he asked me. 'The first time you cried about her?'

"I hadn't thought about it, but it was true.

"Mrs. Trace said, 'Oh, shit.'

"Then the two of them, they just looked at me. I thought they would never say another word until Mrs. Trace said, 'Come to supper, why don't you. Friday evening. You like catfish?'

"I said sure, but I wasn't going to. The hell with the ring. But the Thursday before, I thought about the way Mr. Trace looked at me and the way his wife said 'me.'

"The way she said it. Not like the 'me' was some tough somebody, or somebody she had put together for show. But like, like somebody she favored and could count on. A secret somebody you didn't have to feel sorry for or have to fight for. Somebody who wouldn't have to steal a ring to get back at whitepeople and then lie and say it was a present from them. I wanted the ring back not just because my mother asks me have I found it yet. It's beautiful. But although it belongs to me, it's not mine. I love it, but there's a trick in it, and I have to agree to the trick to say it's mine. Reminds me of the tricky blond kid living inside Mrs. Trace's head. A present taken from whitefolks, given to me when I was too young to say No thank you.

"It was buried with her. That's what I found out when I went back for the catfish supper. Mrs. Trace saw it on Dorcas' hand when she stabbed her in the coffin.

"I had a funny feeling in my stomach, and my throat was too dry to swallow, but I had to ask her just the same—why did she mess up the funeral that way. Mr. Trace looked at her as though he had asked the question.

" 'Lost the lady,' she said. 'Put her down someplace and forgot where.'

" 'How did you find her?'

" 'Looked.'

"We sat there for a while nobody saying anything. Then Mrs. Trace got up to answer a knock at the door. I heard voices. 'Just right here and right here. Won't take but two minutes.'

" 'I don't do no two-minute work.'

" 'Please, Violet, I wouldn't ask if it wasn't absolutely necessary, you know that.'

"They came into the dining room, Mrs. Trace and a woman pleading for a few curls 'just here and here. And maybe you can turn it down up here. Not curled, just turned, know what I mean?'

" 'You all go up front, I won't be too long.' She said that to Mr. Trace and me after we said 'Evening' to the hurry-up customer, but nobody introduced anybody.

"Mr. Trace didn't sit at the window this time. He sat next to me on the sofa.

" 'Felice. That means happy. Are you?'

" 'Sure. No.'

" 'Dorcas wasn't ugly. Inside or out.'

"I shrugged. 'She used people.'

" 'Only if they wanted her to.'

" 'Did you want her to use you?'

" 'Must have.'

" 'Well, I didn't. Thank God she can't anymore.'

"I wished I hadn't taken my sweater off. My dress stretches across the top no matter what I do. He was looking at my face, not my body, so I don't know why I was nervous alone in the room with him.

"Then he said, 'You mad cause she's dead. So am I.'

" 'You the reason she is.'

" 'I know. I know.'

" 'Even if you didn't kill her outright; even if she made herself die, it was you.'

" 'It was me. For the rest of my life, it'll be me. Tell you something. I never saw a needier creature in my life.'

" 'Dorcas? You mean you still stuck on her?'

" 'Stuck? Well, if you mean did I like what I felt about her. I guess I'm stuck to that.'

" 'What about Mrs. Trace? What about her?'

" 'We working on it. Faster now, since you stopped by and told us what you did.'

" 'Dorcas was cold,' I said. 'All the way to the last she was dry-eyed. I never saw her shed a tear about anything.'

"He said, 'I did. You know the hard part of her; I saw the soft. My luck was to tend to it.'

" 'Dorcas? Soft?'

" 'Dorcas. Soft. The girl I knew. Just cause she had scales don't mean she wasn't fry. Nobody knew her that way but me. Nobody tried to love her before me.'

" 'Why'd you shoot at her if you loved her?'

" 'Scared. Didn't know how to love anybody.'

" 'You know now?'

" 'No. Do you, Felice?'

" 'I got other things to do with my time.'

"He didn't laugh at me, so I said, 'I didn't tell you everything.'

" 'There's more?'

" 'I suppose I should. It was the last thing she said. Before she . . . went to sleep. Everybody was screaming, "Who shot you, who did it?" She said, "Leave me alone. I'll tell you tomorrow." She must have thought she was going to be around tomorrow and made me think so too. Then she called my name although I was kneeling right beside her. "Felice. Felice. Come close, closer." I put my face right there. I could smell the fruity liquor on her breath. She was sweating, and whispering to herself. Couldn't keep her eyes open. Then she opened them wide and said real loud: "There's only one apple." Sounded like "apple." "Just one. Tell Joe."

" 'See? You were the last thing on her mind. I was right there, right there. Her best friend, I thought, but not best enough for her to want to go to the emergency room and stay alive. She let herself die right out from under me with my ring and everything and I wasn't even on her mind. So. That's it. I told you.'

"That was the second time I saw him smile but it was more sad than pleased.

" 'Felice,' he said. And kept on saying it. 'Felice. Felice.' With two syllables, not one like most people do, including my father.

"The curled-hair woman came past on her way out the door, chattering, saying, Thanks so much see you Joe sorry to interrupt bye honey didn't catch your name you a blessing Violet a real blessing bye.

"I said I had to go too. Mrs. Trace plopped down in a chair with her head thrown back and her arms dangling. 'People are mean,' she said. 'Plain mean.'

"Mr. Trace said, 'No. Comic is what they are.'

"He laughed a little then, to prove his point, and she did too. I laughed too but it didn't come out right because I didn't think the woman was all that funny.

"Somebody in the house across the alley put a record on and the music floated in to us through the open window. Mr. Trace moved his head to the rhythm and his wife snapped her fingers in time. She did a little step in front of him and he smiled. By and by they were dancing. Funny, like old people do, and I laughed for real. Not because of how funny they looked. Something in it made me feel I shouldn't be there. Shouldn't be looking at them doing that.

"Mr. Trace said, 'Come on, Felice. Let's see what you can do.' He held out his hand.

"Mrs. Trace said, 'Yeah. Come on. Hurry; it's almost over.'

"I shook my head, but I wanted to.

"When they finished and I asked for my sweater, Mrs. Trace said, 'Come back anytime. I want to do your hair for you anyway. Free. Your ends need clipping.'

"Mr. Trace sat down and stretched. 'This place needs birds.'

" 'And a Victrola.'

" 'Watch your mouth, girl.'

" 'If you get one, I'll bring some records. When I come to get my hair done.'

" 'Hear that, Joe? She'll bring some records.'

" 'Then I best find me another job.' He turned tome, touching my elbow as I walked to the door. 'Felice. They named you right. Remember that.'

"I'll tell my mother the truth. I know she is proud of stealing that opal; of daring to do something like that to get back at the whiteman who thought she was stealing even when she wasn't. My mother is so honest she makes people laugh. Returning a pair of gloves to the store when they gave her two pair instead of the one pair she paid for; giving quarters she finds on the seat to conductors on the trolley. It's as though she doesn't live in a big city. When she does stuff like that, my father puts his forehead in his hand and store people and conductor people look at her like she is nutty for sure. So I know how much taking the ring meant to her. How proud she was of breaking her rules for once. But I'll tell her I know about it, and that it's what she did, not the ring, that I really love.

"I'm glad Dorcas has it. It did match her bracelet and matched the house where the party was. The walls were white with silver and turquoise draperies at the windows. The furniture fabric was turquoise too, and the throw rugs the hostess rolled up and put in the spare bedroom were white. Only her dining room was dark and not fixed up like the front part. She probably hadn't got around to doing it over in her favorite colors and let a bowl of Christmas oranges be the only decoration. Her own bedroom was white and gold, but the bedroom she put Dorcas in, a spare one off the dark dining room, was plain.

"I didn't have a fellow for the party. I went along with Dorcas and Acton. Dorcas needed an alibi and I was it. We had just renewed our friendship after she stopped seeing Mr. Trace and was running around with her 'catch.' Somebody a lot of girls older than us wanted and had too. Dorcas liked that part—that other girls were jealous; that he chose her over them; that she had won. That's what she said. 'I won him. I won!' God. You'd think she had been in a fight.

"What the hell did she win? He treated her bad, but she didn't think so. She spent her time figuring out how to keep him interested in her. Plotting what she would do to any girl who tried to move in. That's the way all the girls I know think: how to get, then hold on to, a guy and most of that is having friends who want you to have him, and enemies who don't. I guess that's the way you have to think about it. But what if I don't want to?

"It's warm tonight. Maybe there won't be a spring and we'll slide right on into summer. My mother will like that—she can't stand the cold—and my father, chasing around looking for colored baseball players 'in the flesh and on the lot,' hollering, jumping up and down when he recounts the plays to his friends, he'll be happy too. No blossoms are on the trees yet but it's warm enough. They'll be out soon. That one over there is aching for it. It's not a man tree; I think it's a child. Well, could be a woman, I suppose.

"Her catfish was pretty good. Not as good as the way my grandmother used to do it, or my mother used to before her chest wore out. Too much hot pepper in the dredging flour the way Mrs. Trace fixed it. I drank a lot of water so as not to hurt her feelings. It eased the pain."

Pain. I seem to have an affection, a kind of sweettooth for it. Bolts of lightning, little rivulets of thunder. And I the eye of the storm. Mourning the split trees, hens starving on rooftops. Figuring out what can be done to save them since they cannot save themselves without me because—well, it's my storm, isn't it? I break lives to prove I can mend them back again. And although the pain is theirs, I share it, don't I? Of course. Of course. I wouldn't have it any other way. But it is another way. I am uneasy now. Feeling a bit false. What, I wonder, what would I be without a few brilliant spots of blood to ponder? Without aching words that set, then miss, the mark?

I ought to get out of this place. Avoid the window; leave the hole I cut through the door to get in lives instead of having one of my own. It was loving the City that distracted me and gave me ideas. Made me think I could speak its loud voice and make that sound sound human. I missed the people altogether.

I thought I knew them and wasn't worried that they didn't really know about me. Now it's clear why they contradicted me at every turn: they knew me all along. Out of the corners of their eyes they watched me. And when I was feeling most invisible, being tight-lipped, silent and unobservable, they were whispering about me to each other. They knew how little I could be counted on; how poorly, how shabbily my know-it-all self covered helplessness. That when I invented stories about them—and doing it seemed to me so fine—I was completely in their hands, managed without mercy. I thought I'd hidden myself so well as I watched them through windows and doors, took every opportunity I had to follow them, to gossip about and fill in their lives, and all the while they were watching me. Sometimes they even felt sorry for me and just thinking about their pity I want to die.

So I missed it altogether. I was sure one would kill the other. I waited for it so I could describe it. I was so sure it would happen. That the past was an abused record with no choice but to repeat itself at the crack and no power on earth could lift the arm that held the needle. I was so sure, and they danced and walked all over me. Busy, they were, busy being original, complicated, changeable—human, I guess you'd say, while I was the predictable one, confused in my solitude into arrogance, thinking my space, my view was the only one that was or that mattered. I got so aroused while meddling, while finger-shaping, I overreached and missed the obvious. I was watching the streets, thrilled by the buildings pressing and pressed by stone; so glad to be looking out and in on things I dismissed what went on in heart-pockets closed to me.

I saw the three of them, Felice, Joe and Violet, and they looked to me like a mirror image of Dorcas, Joe and Violet. I believed I saw everything important they did, and based on what I saw I could imagine what I didn't: how exotic they were, how driven. Like dangerous children. That's what I wanted to believe. It never occurred to me that they were thinking other thoughts, feeling other feelings, putting their lives together in ways I never dreamed of. Like Joe. To this moment I'm not sure what his tears were really for, but I do know they were for more than Dorcas. All the while he was running through the streets in bad weather I thought he was looking for her, not Wild's chamber of gold. That home in the rock; that place sunlight got into most of the day. Nothing to be proud of, to show anybody or to want to be in. But I do. I want to be in a place already made for me, both snug and wide open. With a doorway never needing to be closed, a view slanted for light and bright autumn leaves but not rain. Where moonlight can be counted on if the sky is clear and stars no matter what. And below, just yonder, a river called Treason to rely on.

I'd love to close myself in the peace left by the woman who lived there and scared everybody. Unseen because she knows better than to be seen. After all, who would see her, a playful woman who lived in a rock? Who could, without fright? Of her looking eyes looking back? I wouldn't mind. Why should I? She has seen me and is not afraid of me. She hugs me. Understands me. Has given me her hand. I am touched by her. Released in secret.

Now I know.

. . .

Alice Manfred moved away from the tree-lined street back to Springfield. A woman with a taste for brightly colored dresses is there whose breasts are probably soft sealskin purses now, and who may need a few things. Curtains, a good coat lining to bear the winter in. The cheerful company maybe of someone who can provide the necessary things for the night.

Felice still buys Okeh records at Felton's and walks so slowly home from the butcher shop the meat turns before it hits the pan. She thinks that way she can trick me again—moving so slow people nearby seem to be running. Can't fool me: her speed may be slow, but her tempo is next year's news. Whether raised fists freeze in her company or open for a handshake, she's nobody's alibi or hammer or toy.

Joe found work at Paydirt, a speakeasy night job that lets him see the City do its unbelievable sky and run around with Violet in afternoon daylight. On his way home, just after sunrise, he will descend the steps of the Elevated, and if a milk wagon is parked at the curb, he might buy a pint from the second-day crate to cool the evening's hot cornbread supper. When he gets to the apartment building, he picks up the bits of night trash the stoop dwellers have left, drops them in the ashcan and gathers up the children's toys to place them under the stairwell. If he finds a doll he recognizes among the toys, he leaves it propped up and comfortable against the pile. He climbs the stairs and before he gets to his own door he can smell the ham Violet will not give up frying in its own fat to season the hominy swelling in the pot. He calls loudly to her as he closes the door behind him and she calls back: "Vi?" "Joe?" As though it might be another, as though a presumptuous neighbor or a young ghost with bad skin might be there instead. They eat breakfast then and, more often than not, fall asleep. Because of Joe's work—Violet's too—and other things as well, they have stopped night sleeping—exchanging that waste of time for short naps whenever the body insists, and were not surprised by how good they felt. The rest of the day goes however they want it to. After a hairdressing, for example, he meets her at the drugstore for her vanilla malt and his cherry smash.

They walk down 125th Street and across Seventh Avenue and if they get tired they sit down and rest on any stoop they want to and talk weather and youthful misbehavior to the woman leaning on the sill of the first-floor window. Or they might saunter over to the Corner and join the crowd listening to the men with the long-distance eyes. (They like these men, although Violet is worried that one or another of them will tip the wood box or the broken chair he stands on, or that somebody among the group will shout something that hurts the man's feelings. Joe, loving the long-distance eyes, is always supportive and chimes in at appropriate moments with encouraging words.)

Once in a while they take the train all the way to 42nd Street to enjoy what Joe calls the stairway of the lions. Or they idle along 72nd Street to watch men dig holes in the ground for a new building. The deep holes scare Violet, but Joe is fascinated. Both of them think it's a shame.

A lot of the time, though, they stay home figuring things out, telling each other those little personal stories they like to hear again and again, or fussing with the bird Violet bought. She got it cheap because it wasn't well. Hardly any peck to it. Drank water but wouldn't eat. The special bird mix Violet prepared didn't help either. It looked just past her face and didn't turn its head when she tweeted and purred through the bars of the little cage. But, as I said all that time ago, Violet is nothing if not persistent. She guessed the bird wasn't lonely because it was already sad when she bought it out of a flock of others. So if neither food nor company nor its own shelter was important to it, Violet decided, and Joe agreed, nothing was left to love or need but music. They took the cage to the roof one Saturday, where the wind blew and so did the musicians in shirts billowing out behind them. From then on the bird was a pleasure to itself and to them.

Since Joe had to be at work at midnight, they cherished after-supper time. If they did not play bid whist with Gistan and Stuck, and Stuck's new wife, Faye, or promise to keep an eye out for somebody's children, or let Malvonne in to gossip so she wouldn't feel bad about pretending loyalty and betraying them both, they played poker just the two of them until it was time to go to bed under the quilt they plan to tear into its original scraps right soon and get a nice wool blanket with a satin hem. Powder blue, maybe, although that would be risky with the soot flying and all, but Joe is partial to blue. He wants to slip under it and hold on to her. Take her hand and put it on his chest, his stomach. He wants to imagine, as he lies with her in the dark, the shapes their bodies make the blue stuff do. Violet doesn't care what color it is, so long as under their chins that avenue of no-question-about-it satin cools their lava forever.

Lying next to her, his head turned toward the window, he sees through the glass darkness taking the shape of a shoulder with a thin line of blood. Slowly, slowly it forms itself into a bird with a blade of red on the wing. Meanwhile Violet rests her hand on his chest as though it were the sunlit rim of a well and down there somebody is gathering gifts (lead pencils, Bull Durham, Jap Rose Soap) to distribute to them all.

There was an evening, back in 1906, before Joe and Violet went to the City, when Violet left the plow and walked into their little shotgun house, the heat of the day still stunning. She was wearing coveralls and a sleeveless faded shirt and slowly removed them along with the cloth from her head. On a table near the cookstove stood an enamel basin—speckled blue and white and chipped all round its rim. Under a square of toweling, placed there to keep insects out, the basin was full of still water. Palms up, fingers leading, Violet slid her hands into the water and rinsed her face. Several times she scooped and splashed until, perspiration and water mixed, her cheeks and forehead cooled. Then, dipping the toweling into the water, carefully she bathed. From the windowsill she took a white shift, laundered that very morning, and dropped it over her head and shoulders. Finally she sat on the bed to unwind her hair. Most of the knots fixed that morning had loosened under her headcloth and were now cupfuls of soft wool her fingers thrilled to. Sitting there, her hands deep in the forbidden pleasure of her hair, she noticed she had not removed her heavy work shoes. Putting the toe of her left foot to the heel of the right, she pushed the shoe off. The effort seemed extra and the mild surprise at how very tired she felt was interrupted by a soft, wide hat, as worn and dim as the room she sat in, descending on her. Violet did not feel her shoulder touch the mattress. Way before that she had entered a safe sleep. Deep, trustworthy, feathered in colored dreams. The heat was relentless, insinuating. Like the voices of the women in houses nearby singing "Go down, go down, way down in Egypt land . . ." Answering each other from yard to yard with a verse or its variation.

Joe had been away for two months at Crossland, and when he got home and stood in the doorway, he saw Violet's dark girl-body limp on the bed. She looked frail to him, and penetrable everyplace except at one foot, the left, where her man's work shoe remained. Smiling, he took off his straw hat and sat down at the bottom of the bed. One of her hands held her face; the other rested on her thigh. He looked at the fingernails hard as her palm skin, and noticed for the first time how shapely her hands were. The arm that curved out of the shift's white sleeve was muscled by field labor, awful thin, but smooth as a child's. He undid the laces of her shoe and eased it off. It must have helped something in her dream for she laughed then, a light happy laugh that he had never heard before, but which seemed to belong to her.

When I see them now they are not sepia, still, losing their edges to the light of a future afternoon. Caught midway between was and must be. For me they are real. Sharply in focus and clicking. I wonder, do they know they are the sound of snapping fingers under the sycamores lining the streets? When the loud trains pull into their stops and the engines pause, attentive listeners can hear it. Even when they are not there, when whole city blocks downtown and acres of lawned neighborhoods in Sag Harbor cannot see them, the clicking is there.

In the T-strap shoes of Long Island debutantes, the sparkling fringes of daring short skirts that swish and glide to music that intoxicates them more than the champagne. It is in the eyes of the old men who watch these girls, and the young ones who hold them up. It is in the graceful slouch of the men slipping their hands into the pockets of their tuxedo trousers. Their teeth are bright; their hair is smooth and parted in the middle. And when they take the arms of the T-strap girls and guide them away from the crowd and the too-bright lights, it is the clicking that makes them sway on unlit porches while the Victrola plays in the parlor. The click of dark and snapping fingers drives them to Roseland, to Bunny's; boardwalks by the sea. Into places their fathers have warned them about and their mothers shudder to think of. Both the warning and the shudder come from the snapping fingers, the clicking. And the shade. Pushed away into certain streets, restricted from others, making it possible for the inhabitants to sigh and sleep in relief, the shade stretches—just there—at the edge of the dream, or slips into the crevices of a chuckle. It is out there in the privet hedge that lines the avenue. Gliding through rooms as though it is tidying this, straightening that. It bunches on the curbstone, wrists crossed, and hides its smile under a wide-brim hat. Shade. Protective, available. Or sometimes not; sometimes it seems to lurk rather than hover kindly, and its stretch is not a yawn but an increase to be beaten back with a stick. Before it clicks, or taps or snaps its fingers.

Some of them know it. The lucky ones. Everywhere they go they are like a magician-made clock with hands the same size so you can't figure out what time it is, but you can hear the ticking, tap, snap.

I started out believing that life was made just so the world would have some way to think about itself, but that it had gone awry with humans because flesh, pinioned by misery, hangs on to it with pleasure. Hangs on to wells and a boy's golden hair; would just as soon inhale sweet fire caused by a burning girl as hold a maybe-yes maybe-no hand. I don't believe that anymore. Something is missing there. Something rogue. Something else you have to figure in before you can figure it out.

It's nice when grown people whisper to each other under the covers. Their ecstasy is more leaf-sigh than bray and the body is the vehicle, not the point. They reach, grown people, for something beyond, way beyond and way, way down underneath tissue. They are remembering while they whisper the carnival dolls they won and the Baltimore boats they never sailed on. The pears they let hang on the limb because if they plucked them, they would be gone from there and who else would see that ripeness if they took it away for themselves? How could anybody passing by see them and imagine for themselves what the flavor would be like? Breathing and murmuring under covers both of them have washed and hung out on the line, in a bed they chose together and kept together nevermind one leg was propped on a 1916 dictionary, and the mattress, curved like a preacher's palm asking for witnesses in His name's sake, enclosed them each and every night and muffled their whispering, old-time love. They are under the covers because they don't have to look at themselves anymore; there is no stud's eye, no chippie glance to undo them. They are inward toward the other, bound and joined by carnival dolls and the steamers that sailed from ports they never saw. That is what is beneath their undercover whispers.

But there is another part, not so secret. The part that touches fingers when one passes the cup and saucer to the other. The part that closes her neckline snap while waiting for the trolley; and brushes lint from his blue serge suit when they come out of the movie house into the sunlight.

I envy them their public love. I myself have only known it in secret, shared it in secret and longed, aw longed to show it—to be able to say out loud what they have no need to say at all: *That I have loved only you, surrendered my whole self reckless to you and nobody else. That I want you to love me back and show it to me. That I love the way you hold me, how close you let me be to you. I like your fingers on and on, lifting, turning. I have watched your face for a long time now, and missed your eyes when you went away from me. Talking to you and hearing you answer—that's the kick.*

But I can't say that aloud; I can't tell anyone that I have been waiting for this all my life and that being chosen to wait is the reason I can. If I were able I'd say it. Say make me, remake me. You are free to do it and I am free to let you because look, look. Look where your hands are. Now.

# ALSO BY TONI MORRISON

## BELOVED

Morrison's Pulitzer Prize–winning *Beloved* is the story of Sethe, an escaped slave, who has lost a husband and buried a child. She now lives in a small house on the edge of town with her daughter, Denver, her mother-in-law, and a disturbing, mesmerizing apparition called Beloved. Though Sethe works at "beating back the past," it makes itself heard and felt incessantly, most especially through Beloved, whose childhood belongs to the hideous logic of slavery and who has now returned from the "place over there" to exact retribution for what she lost and for what was taken from her.

Fiction/Literature/1-4000-3341-1

## SONG OF SOLOMON

*Song of Solomon*, a novel of great beauty and power, creates a magical world out of four generations of black life in America, with the birth of Macon Dead, Jr., known as Milkman, son of the richest black family in a Midwestern town. Milkman grows up in his father's money-haunted, death-haunted house and then strikes out alone toward adventure, and as the unspoken truth about his family and his buried heritage comes to light, toward an adventurous and crucial embrace of life.

Fiction/Literature/1-4000-3342-X

## SULA

Both black, both smart, both poor, and raised in a small Ohio town, Sula and Nel meet when they are twelve, wishbone thin and dreaming of princes. Through their girlhood years they share everything until Sula escapes the Bottom, their hilltop neighborhood of fierce resentment toward failed crops, lost jobs, thieving insurance men, and bug-ridden flour. Sula roams the cities of America for ten years, and when she returns to town she finds Nel married and acculturated to life at the Bottom, while Sula remains the oddity of the community.

Fiction/Literature/1-4000-3343-8

## TAR BABY

The cultivated millionaire Valerian Street's existence is arranged by his fastidious butler, Sydney, whose niece Jadine has been educated at the Sorbonne at Valerian's expense. One night, a ragged, starving black American street man breaks into the house. Jadine, who at first is repelled by the intruder, finds herself moving inexorably toward him; he is a kind of black man she has dreaded since childhood: uneducated, violent, and contemptuous of her privilege. Each becomes fascinated with the other, and the novel deftly reveals how the conflicts and dramas wrought by social and cultural circumstances must ultimately be played out in the realm of the heart.

Fiction/Literature/1-4000-3344-6

## PLAYING IN THE DARK

*Whiteness and the Literary Imagination*

Toni Morrison's brilliant discussions of the "Africanist" presence in the fiction of Poe, Melville, Cather, and Hemingway lead to a dramatic reappraisal of the essential characteristics of our literary tradition. She shows how much the themes of freedom and individualism, manhood and innocence, depended on the existence of a black population that was manifestly unfree, which came to serve white authors as embodiments of their own fears and desires.

Literary Criticism/0-679-74542-4

VINTAGE BOOKS
Available at your local bookstore, or call toll-free to order:
1-800-793-2665 (credit cards only)

31901064521653